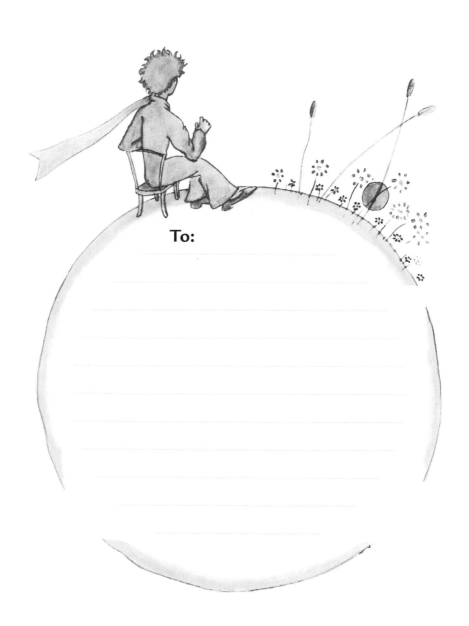

To:
_____
_____
_____
_____
_____
_____
_____
_____

寫・小王子

透過手抄、慢讀，打開心靈的眼睛，
藉由書寫，體驗「寫下來」帶來的改變

安東尼・聖修伯里
Antoine de Saint-Exupéry ／著

墨丸／譯

閱讀小王子的另一種方法

漫遊者文化編輯部

《小王子》（法語：Le Petit Prince，英語：The Little Prince）自 1943 年出版以來，幾乎可以說是地球上最受歡迎的讀物，賣出近 2 億冊，有 250 多種的翻譯版本。

大多數人可能都知道《小王子》的大概故事（就是小王子跟他的玫瑰花，還有一隻聰明的狐狸），也可能在學生時代被師長要求讀這本書（甚至還寫過讀書報告），但你真的讀懂了這個故事蘊含的寓意嗎？

近幾年來，透過「用筆書寫」這個行為或者說做為某種方法，確實幫助許多人，達到心想事成的目的，可能是提高了創作力，可能是改善了表達方式，可能是療癒了自己的心靈。

這一次，出版《寫 · 小王子》，我們確實想透過手抄 · 慢讀，讓美好的事物，漂亮的句子，他人的生活經驗，在書寫的過程中停留在你的腦中，讓這些轉化成你獨有的表述方式， 體驗到「寫下來」帶來的改變。

《寫‧小王子》的推薦使用法（一）：寫中文/英文

抄寫經典名作的文字，是許多作家增進寫作能力的秘訣，不論是書寫英文還是中文，只要每天堅持寫，都同樣能提高語言能力。

用眼睛讀，然後專心的寫下每一個字。

寫中文，目的是增強閱讀跟理解力。

寫英文，用來增加英文字彙跟表述能力。

《寫‧小王子》的推薦使用法（二）：寫金句

《小王子》受到這麼多人的喜愛，除了故事呼應了讀者的心情，更重要的是，小王子說出的話，或許有深刻的哲理或許有眞摯的情誼，這些句子觸動了我們內心深處最溫柔的情感。

寫下你喜歡的句子，讓它伴隨你度過每一個心情轉折的時刻。

寫金句，讓感動伴隨你長久。

獻給里昂‧維赫特

孩子們，請原諒我把這本書獻給一個大人。我有個很重要的理由：這個大人是我在世界上最好的朋友。還有一個理由是：這個大人什麼都懂，就算是寫給孩子看的書他也懂。第三個理由是：這個大人住在法國，他正飢寒交迫，非常需要安慰。如果以上理由還是不能說服大家，那我就把這本書獻給這個大人的童年。

每一個大人都曾經是個小孩。（可惜，記得這件事的大人實在不多。）所以，我把獻詞改為：

獻給小男孩時代的里昂‧維赫特

To Leon Werth

I ask the indulgence of the children who may read this book for dedicating it to a grown-up. I have a serious reason: he is the best friend I have in the world. I have another reason: this grown-up understands everything, even books about children. I have a third reason: he lives in France where he is hungry and cold. He needs cheering up. If all these reasons are not enough, I will dedicate the book to the child from whom this grown-up grew.

All grown-ups were once children—although few of them remember it. And so I correct my dedication:

To Leon Werth
when he was a little boy

1

　　在我六歲的時候，從《真實歷險》這本描繪原始森林的書裡，看過一幅精彩的插圖，有條蟒蛇正準備吞食一隻巨大的野獸。底下就是那張圖的副本。

　　書裡面寫著：「蟒蛇一口都不嚼直接把獵物囫圇吞進腹中，接下來就無法動彈。牠們會在長達六個月的睡眠中慢慢消化獵物。」

Once when I was six years old I saw a magnificent picture in a book, called True Stories from Nature, about the primeval forest. It was a picture of a boa constrictor in the act of swallowing an animal. Here is a copy of the drawing.

In the book it said: "Boa constrictors swallow their prey whole, without chewing it. After that they are not able to move, and they sleep through the six months that they need for digestion."

我對叢林冒險抱有各式各樣的幻想，所以我拿起彩色鉛筆畫了生平第一幅圖。我的第一號作品，看起來像這樣。

我把這幅傑作拿給大人看，問他們會不會覺得很可怕。

但是他們卻回答：「一頂帽子有什麼好怕的？」

這才不是帽子，是一條巨蟒正在消化肚子裡的大象。然後我把巨蟒肚子裡的樣子畫出來，讓大人看得更清楚。

這些大人，總是要把東西明明白白解釋給他們聽才行。

I pondered deeply, then, over the adventures of the jungle. And after some work with a colored pencil I succeeded in making my first drawing. My Drawing Number One. It looked like this.

I showed my masterpiece to the grown-ups, and asked them whether the drawing frightened them.

But they answered: "Frighten? Why should any one be frightened by a hat?"

My drawing was not a picture of a hat. It was a picture of a boa constrictor digesting an elephant. But since the grown-ups were not able to understand it, I made another drawing: I drew the inside of the boa constrictor, so that the grown-ups could see it clearly. They always need to have things explained.

我的第二號作品長得像這樣

這次，大人勸我別再畫這些吃飽喝足的蟒蛇，肚子裡的東西有沒有畫出來根本無所謂；我應該把精神放在地理、歷史、數學、文法這些科目上。

就這樣，我在六歲那年放棄了畫家這個美好的職業。我的第一號和第二號作品接連失敗，也讓我十分沮喪。

大人從來不願意自己花精神去了解，總是要小孩解釋給他們聽，真是累人。

後來我選擇另一種職業，我學會開飛機，幾乎飛遍世界各個角落。地理知識發揮了很大的作用。我一眼就能辨別中國和亞利桑那有何不同。如果在黑夜中迷失方向，地理真的相當實用。

My Drawing Number Two looked like this:

The grown-ups' response, this time, was to advise me to lay aside my drawings of boa constrictors, whether from the inside or the outside, and devote myself instead to geography, history, arithmetic and grammar.

That is why, at the age of six, I gave up what might have been a magnificent career as a painter. I had been disheartened by the failure of my Drawing Number One and my Drawing Number Two.

Grown-ups never understand anything by themselves, and it is tiresome for children to be always and forever explaining things to them.

So then I chose another profession, and learned to pilot airplanes. I have flown a little over all parts of the world; and it is true that geography has been very useful to me. At a glance I can distinguish China from Arizona. If one gets lost in the night, such knowledge is valuable.

也因為四處飛行的生活，我遇過很多嚴肅認真的人。我跟大人一起生活過很長的時間，仔細觀察過他們，但是我對他們的看法卻依然沒有多大改變。

每當我遇到一個看起來腦筋清楚的大人，就會拿出小心保存的第一號作品來試試他。我想知道他能否看懂這幅畫。不過，他們的回答總是：「這是帽子。」

所以我也不會和他談巨蟒、叢林，或是星星之類的話題。我會降低自己的水準，跟他們聊聊橋牌、高爾夫球，或是政治、領帶這些東西。最後，這個大人會非常高興能認識像我這樣講理的人。

In the course of this life I have had a great many encounters with a great many people who have been concerned with matters of consequence. I have lived a great deal among grown-ups. I have seen them intimately, close at hand. And that hasn't much improved my opinion of them.

Whenever I met one of them who seemed to me at all clear-sighted, I tried the experiment of showing him my Drawing Number One, which I have always kept. I would try to find out, so, if this was a person of true understanding. But, whoever it was, he, or she, would always say: "That is a hat."

Then I would never talk to that person about boa constrictors, or primeval forests, or stars. I would bring myself down to his level. I would talk to him about bridge, and golf, and politics, and neckties. And the grown-up would be greatly pleased to have met such a sensible man.

2

我就這樣獨自生活，身邊連個能說真心話的人都沒有，直到六年前在撒哈拉沙漠裡飛機失事。飛機引擎裡有個東西壞了。

當時機上沒帶維修員也沒帶旅客，我只能試著一個人完成困難重重的修理工作。對我來說這事關生死。我身上的水只剩下一星期的份。

第一天晚上，我在距離人煙千里的大沙漠上入睡，比汪洋中趴在竹筏上的遇難者還要孤獨得多。

因此第二天清晨，我被一個怪異細小的聲音喚醒的時候，你可以想像我有多麼驚訝。

So I lived my life alone, without anyone that I could really talk to, until I had an accident with my plane in the Desert of Sahara, six years ago. Something was broken in my engine.

And as I had with me neither a mechanic nor any passengers, I set myself to attempt the difficult repairs all alone. It was a question of life or death for me: I had scarcely enough drinking water to last a week.

The first night, then, I went to sleep on the sand, a thousand miles from any human habitation. I was more isolated than a shipwrecked sailor on a raft in the middle of the ocean.

Thus you can imagine my amazement, at sunrise, when I was awakened by an odd little voice.

小小的聲音說：

「請你……畫一隻羊給我。」

「啊！」

「畫一隻羊給我……」

我像是被雷擊中似的，整個人跳了起來。我用力揉揉眼睛，仔細地四下觀望。

我看見一個非比尋常的小人兒，他正認真地盯著我瞧。這是後來我畫他畫得最好的一幅肖像畫，當然比起模特兒本人，這幅圖是遜色太多了。

It said:

"If you please—draw me a sheep!"

"What!"

"Draw me a sheep!"

I jumped to my feet, completely thunderstruck. I blinked my eyes hard. I looked carefully all around me.

And I saw a most extraordinary small person, who stood there examining me with great seriousness. Here you may see the best potrait that, later, I was able to make of him. But my drawing is certainly very much less charming than its model.

這不能怪我。那些大人的反應，讓我在六歲的時候就放棄了畫家這條路，除了畫過一條吃飽喝足的蟒蛇和一條看得見肚子裡裝什麼的蟒蛇，我再沒動過筆。

我瞪大眼睛訝異地看著這突然現身的小人兒。

別忘了，我當時在和人間相隔千里的沙漠裡。這個小人兒不像是迷路，看上去也沒有一點飢渴疲憊，或是害怕的模樣。他絲毫不像是在距離人煙千里之外的大沙漠中跟誰走丟了。我終於擺脫驚訝，能夠開口說話的時候，對他說了一句：

「你在這裡幹什麼？」

That, however, is not my fault. The grown-ups discouraged me in my painter's career when I was six years old, and I never learned to draw anything, except boas from the outside and boas from the inside.

Now I stared at this sudden apparition with my eyes fairly starting out of my head in astonishment.

Remember, I had crashed in the desert a thousand miles from any inhabited region. And yet my little man seemed neither to be straying uncertainly among the sands, nor to be fainting from fatigue or hunger or thirst or fear. Nothing about him gave any suggestion of a child lost in the middle of the desert, a thousand miles from any human habitation. When at last I was able to speak, I said to him:

"But—what are you doing here?"

他卻彷彿有什麼重要的事一般，緩緩地再說了一次：

「請你……畫一隻羊給我……」

當神祕的力量太過強大的時候，沒有人能夠拒絕臣服於它。杳無人煙的沙漠上，我正面臨死亡的危機，卻還是拿出了一張紙和一枝筆，無論這個舉動有多麼荒誕不經。突然間我想起自己這輩子最專精的是地理、歷史、數學和文法，就有點生氣地對小人兒說我不會畫畫。他回答：

「沒關係，畫一隻羊給我吧！」

我從沒畫過羊，所以就在我生平唯二會畫的兩張圖當中，選了吃飽喝足的蟒蛇畫給他。沒想到，這小人兒的回答讓我瞠目結舌。

And in answer he repeated, very slowly, as if he were speaking of a matter of great consequence: "If you please—draw me a sheep…"

When a mystery is too overpowering, one dare not disobey. Absurd as it might seem to me, a thousand miles from any human habitation and in danger of death, I took out of my pocket a sheet of paper and my fountain-pen. But then I remembered how my studies had been concentrated on geography, history, arithmetic, and grammar, and I told the little chap (a little crossly, too) that I did not know how to draw. He answered me:

"That doesn't matter. Draw me a sheep…"

But I had never drawn a sheep. So I drew for him one of the two pictures I had drawn so often. It was that of the boa constrictor from the outside. And I was astounded to hear the little fellow greet it with,

「不、不！我不要肚子裡有一頭大象的蟒蛇。蟒蛇太危險，大象又太占空間。我住的地方很小，我想要一隻羊。畫一隻羊給我吧。」

於是，我畫了一隻羊給他。

他專心看著羊，然後說：

「不！這是一隻生了重病的羊。再畫一隻給我。」

我又動了筆。

這次我的朋友微微一笑，有些不置可否：「看你畫的，這不是綿羊，而是隻公羊，牠頭上還長著角呢。」

然後我再畫了一隻羊。

跟前幾隻一樣，他還是不要。

「這隻羊太老了。我想要一隻長壽的羊。」

"No, no, no! I do not want an elephant inside a boa constrictor. A boa constrictor is a very dangerous creature, and an elephant is very cumbersome. Where I live, everything is very small. What I need is a sheep. Draw me a sheep."

So then I made a drawing.

He looked at it carefully, then he said:

"No. This sheep is already very sickly. Make me another."

So I made another drawing.

My friend smiled gently and indulgenty.

"You see yourself," he said, "that this is not a sheep. This is a ram. It has horns."

So then I did my drawing over once more.

But it was rejected too, just like the others.

"This one is too old. I want a sheep that will live a long time."

他耗盡了我的耐心，我急著修理引擎，就草草畫了一張圖。
而且隨便解釋說：

「這是個箱子，你要的羊就在裡面。」

沒想到這位年輕的小評審卻意外地笑逐顏開。他說：

「這就是我要的……你覺得這隻羊會需要很多草嗎？」

「為什麼？」

「因為我住的地方很小很小……」

「一定夠！我畫的是一隻很小很小的羊。」

他把臉湊到畫前面。

「也沒那麼小……看！牠睡著了……」

就這樣，我認識了小王子。

By this time my patience was exhausted, because I was in a hurry to start taking my engine apart. So I tossed off this drawing.

And I threw out an explanation with it.

"This is only his box. The sheep you asked for is inside."

I was very surprised to see a light break over the face of my young judge:

"That is exactly the way I wanted it! Do you think that this sheep will have to have a great deal of grass?"

"Why?"

"Because where I live everything is very small…"

"There will surely be enough grass for him," I said. "It is a very small sheep that I have given you."

He bent his head over the drawing:

"Not so small that—Look! He has gone to sleep…"

And that is how I made the acquaintance of the little prince.

3

　過了好久，我才搞清楚他來自哪裡。小王子向我頻頻發問，但他對於我的種種疑問，卻好像根本沒聽見似的。我是慢慢從我們交談的隻字片語中，一點一點拼湊出小王子的一切。

　比如說，他第一次看到我的飛機時（我就不把飛機畫出來了，這對我來說實在太複雜），他問道：

　「這是什麼東西？」

　「這不是『東西』，它會飛。這是飛機，我的飛機。」

　我十分驕傲地告訴小王子我會飛。

It took me a long time to learn where he came from. The little prince, who asked me so many questions, never seemed to hear the ones I asked him. It was from words dropped by chance that, little by little, everything was revealed to me.

The first time he saw my airplane, for instance (I shall not draw my airplane; that would be much too complicated for me), he asked me:

"What is that object?"

"That is not an object. It flies. It is an airplane. It is my airplane."

And I was proud to have him learn that I could fly.

他大聲喊道：

「什麼？你是從天上掉下來的？」

「是的。」我謙虛地回答。

「啊？真奇怪。」

小王子發出一陣銀鈴般的笑聲，讓我很是惱火。我希望別人認真看待我的不幸。

他又說：「那你也是從天上來的！你的星球是哪個？」

剎那間，小王子現身於此的謎團透出一絲光明。我脫口而出：

「你是從另一個星球上來的嗎？」

他沒有回答這個問題。他緩緩地搖了搖頭，邊盯著我的飛機看，接著說：

「也是，你坐著這個東西，不可能是從很遠很遠的地方來的……」

He cried out, then:

"What! You dropped down from the sky?"

"Yes," I answered, modestly.

"Oh! That is funny!"

And the little prince broke into a lovely peal of laughter, which irritated me very much. I like my misfortunes to be taken seriously.

Then he added: "So you, too, come from the sky! Which is your planet?"

At that moment I caught a gleam of light in the impenetrable mystery of his presence; and I demanded, abruptly:

"Do you come from another planet?"

But he did not reply. He tossed his head gently, without taking his eyes from my plane:

"It is true that on that you can't have come from very far away..."

然後，他就陷入沉思，久久都有沒回過神來。後來才從口袋裡掏出我畫的小羊，盯著看得入神。

　　你可以想像，「別的星球」這個曖昧不明的話題挑起了我多大的好奇心。我想辦法要多知道一些。

　　「我的小人兒啊，你到底是從哪裡來的？你住在哪裡？你要把我的小羊帶到哪裡去？」

　　他默默想了一會兒，才答道：

　　「幸好你畫了個箱子給我，晚上可以當作小羊的家。」

　　「當然。如果你乖乖的話，我再畫一條繩子給你，白天你可以把羊綁住。再畫一根柱子給你繫繩子。」

And he sank into a reverie, which lasted a long time. Then, taking my sheep out of his pocket, he buried himself in the contemplation of his treasure.

You can imagine how my curiosity was aroused by this half-confidence about the "other planets." I made a great effort, therefore, to find out more on this subject.

"My little man, where do you come from? What is this 'where I live,' of which you speak? Where do you want to take your sheep?"

After a reflective silence he answered:

"The thing that is so good about the box you have given me is that at night he can use it as his house."

"That is so. And if you are good I will give you a string, too, so that you can tie him during the day, and a post to tie him to."

我的建議似乎讓小王子有些反感。

「綁住牠？好怪的想法。」

「你要是不把牠綁住，牠會四處跑，萬一牠走丟了……」

我的朋友又笑了起來：

「你以為牠能跑去哪裡呀？」

「牠哪裡都會去，牠會一直往前跑……」

小王子認真地說：

「沒關係，我住的地方很小很小。」

然後，他略帶傷感地又補了一句：

「一直往前跑，也去不了多遠……」

But the little prince seemed shocked by this offer:

"Tie him! What a queer idea!"

"But if you don't tie him," I said, "he will wander off somewhere, and get lost."

My friend broke into another peal of laughter:

"But where do you think he would go?"

"Anywhere. Straight ahead of him."

Then the little prince said, earnestly:

"That doesn't matter. Where I live, everything is so small!"

And, with perhaps a hint of sadness, he added:

"Straight ahead of him, nobody can go very far…"

4

　我知道的關於小王子第二件重要的事，就是他住的星球比一棟房子大不了多少。

　沒什麼好吃驚的。

　除了地球、木星、火星、金星這幾個曾被命名的大行星以外，我知道宇宙間還存在千百個星球，有些星球太小，就算用望遠鏡也很難看到。每當天文學者發現一顆小星星，他並不會替它命名，只會給它一個編號，例如「325 小行星」。

I had thus learned a second fact of great importance: this was that the planet the little prince came from was scarcely any larger than a house!

But that did not really surprise me much.

I knew very well that in addition to the great planets—such as the Earth, Jupiter, Mars, Venus—to which we have given names, there are also hundreds of others, some of which are so small that one has a hard time seeing them through the telescope. When an astronomer discovers one of these he does not give it a name, but only a number. He might call it, for example, "Asteroid 325."

我有確切的理由相信，小王子住的星球就是 B612 小行星。

I have serious reason to believe that the planet from which the little prince came is the asteroid known as B-612.

這顆小行星，只有一九〇九年一位土耳其天文學家曾在望遠鏡裡看過一次。

他在國際太空大會上發表關於這項發現的演說。但他穿了一身土耳其傳統服裝上台，所以沒有一個人相信他說的話。

大人就是這樣。

幸好，土耳其的獨裁者為了挽回 B612 星球的名聲，強迫土耳其人民都要改穿歐洲服飾，否則就處以死刑。一九二〇年，這位天文學家穿上一身優雅迷人的西服，再次發表演說。這次每個人都對他說的話深信不疑。

This asteroid has only once been seen through the telescope. That was by a Turkish astronomer, in 1909.

On making his discovery, the astronomer had presented it to the International Astronomical Congress, in a great demonstration. But he was in Turkish costume, and so nobody would believe what he said.

Grown-ups are like that…

Fortunately, however, for the reputation of Asteroid B-612, a Turkish dictator made a law that his subjects, under pain of death, should change to European costume. So in 1920 the astronomer gave his demonstration all over again, dressed with impressive style and elegance. And this time everybody accepted his report.

如果我告訴你關於 B612 小行星的各種細節，還有它的編號，這都是因為大人老是喜歡這樣做。

大人喜歡數字。當你跟大人提起一個新朋友，他們從來不問真正重要的問題。他們決不會問：「他說話的語調如何？他愛玩什麼遊戲？他收不收集蝴蝶？」

他們只會問：「他幾歲？家裡有幾個兄弟姊妹？他多重？他爸爸賺多少錢？」他們認為知道這些，才算得上了解。

如果你告訴大人：「我看見一幢漂亮房子，磚瓦是玫瑰色的，窗邊擺滿天竺葵，屋頂上還有鴿子……」他們也無法想像。

應該這樣說：「我看見一幢十萬法郎的房子。」他們會大喊：「多美的房子啊！」

If I have told you these details about the asteroid, and made a note of its number for you, it is on account of the grown-ups and their ways.

When you tell them that you have made a new friend, they never ask you any questions about essential matters. They never say to you, "What does his voice sound like? What games does he love best? Does he collect butterflies?"

Instead, they demand: "How old is he? How many brothers has he? How much does he weigh? How much money does his father make?" Only from these figures do they think they have learned anything about him.

If you were to say to the grown-ups: "I saw a beautiful house made of rosy brick, with geraniums in the windows and doves on the roof," they would not be able to get any idea of that house at all.

You would have to say to them: "I saw a house that cost $20,000." Then they would exclaim: "Oh, what a pretty house that is!"

因此，如果你告訴他們：「小王子存在的證據就是他很迷人，他很愛笑，他想要一隻羊。如果有人想要一隻羊，這就足以證明他的存在。」

Just so, you might say to them: "The proof that the little prince existed is that he was charming, that he laughed, and that he was looking for a sheep. If anybody wants a sheep, that is a proof that he exists." And what good would it do to tell them that?

他們只會聳聳肩，把你當作小孩！但是，如果你說：「小王子是從 B612 小行星來的。」就能說服大人，也不會再東問西問來煩你。他們就是這樣。不怪他們，小孩不要對大人太嚴苛。

當然，在我們這些了解何謂人生的人眼裡看來，編號不過是個笑話！

我真想像講個童話故事一般來說這個故事，開頭像這樣：

「從前從前，有一個小王子，住在一個和他差不多大小的星球上，他需要一個朋友……」對於了解人生的人而言，這顯得更為真實。

They would shrug their shoulders, and treat you like a child. But if you said to them: "The planet he came from is Asteroid B-612," then they would be convinced, and leave you in peace from their questions. They are like that. One must not hold it against them. Children should always show great forbearance toward grown-up people.

But certainly, for us who understand life, figures are a matter of indifference.

I should have liked to begin this story in the fashion of the fairy-tales. I should have like to say: "Once upon a time there was a little prince who lived on a planet that was scarcely any bigger than himself, and who had need of a sheep…"

To those who understand life, that would have given a much greater air of truth to my story.

但是我不喜歡別人隨隨便便地讀這本書，因為我在回憶這些往事的時候心裡還很難過。我的朋友和他的小羊已經離開六年了。我寫下他的故事，就是為了不要忘記他。

忘記朋友這種事情太過悲哀，不是每個人都能交到一個朋友。我可能也會變成那種只在乎數字的大人。

因為這種種原因，我買了一盒顏料跟幾枝鉛筆。到我這個年紀，而且還是個只在六歲時畫過兩條蟒蛇就再沒畫過別的東西的人，現在要重回繪畫的懷抱，簡直難如登天！

For I do not want any one to read my book carelessly. I have suffered too much grief in setting down these memories. Six years have already passed since my friend went away from me, with his sheep. If I try to describe him here, it is to make sure that I shall not forget him.

To forget a friend is sad. Not every one has had a friend. And if I forget him, I may become like the grown-ups who are no longer interested in anything but figures...

It is for that purpose, again, that I have bought a box of paints and some pencils. It is hard to take up drawing again at my age, when I have never made any pictures except those of the boa constrictor from the outside and the boa constrictor from the inside, since I was six.

當然，我會努力把最眞實的一面畫下來，但我不能保證自己能夠心想事成。一張畫得還有模有樣，另一張就不怎麼樣了。身材比例，我也掌握得不太好，書裡有的小王子畫得太大，有的又畫得太小。他的衣著顏色也讓我下筆猶豫。於是我東塗塗西改改，畫得不太好也不太壞。的確，最後可能還是有些重要的地方畫錯了，請大家見諒。因爲我的朋友從沒解釋過什麼，他以爲我跟他是一樣的。

但是很遺憾，我一次也沒有看到過盒子裡的小羊。

或許我有點像大人了，我已經變老了。

I shall certainly try to make my portraits as true to life as possible. But I am not at all sure of success. One drawing goes along all right, and another has no resemblance to its subject. I make some errors, too, in the littl e prince's height: in one place he is too tall and in another too short. And I feel some doubts about the color of his costume. So I fumble along as best I can, now good, now bad, and I hope generally fair-to-middling.In certain more important details I shall make mistakes, also. But that is something that will not be my fault. My friend never explained anything to me. He thought, perhaps, that I was like himself.

But I, alas, do not know how to see sheep through t he walls of boxes.

Perhaps I am a little like the grown-ups. I have had to grow old.

5

每一天，我對小王子的星球都會多了解一些，他為何離開以及旅途中發生的事情。這些都是慢慢從他的談話中洩漏出來的。因此，到第三天的時候我知道了關於猴麵包樹的種種。

這次也是由羊的問題起頭，小王子突然很認真地問我：

「羊真的會吃灌木嗎？」

「嗯，會吃。」

「太好了。」

我不懂羊吃灌木為什麼這麼重要。不過小王子又問：

「所以，羊也會吃猴麵包樹嗎？」

As each day passed I would learn, in our talk, something about the little prince's planet, his departure from it, his journey. The information would come very slowly, as it might chance to fall from his thoughts. It was in this way that I heard, on the third day, about the catastrophe of the baobabs.

This time, once more, I had the sheep to thank for it. For the little prince asked me abruptly—as if seized by a grave doubt—

"It is true, isn't it, that sheep eat little bushes?"

"Yes, that is true."

"Ah! I am glad!"

I did not understand why it was so important that sheep should eat little bushes. But the little prince added:

"Then it follows that they also eat baobabs?"

我告訴小王子，猴麵包樹不像灌木那麼小，而是一種跟教堂差不多大的大樹，即使他帶了一群大象回去，也吃不完一棵猴麵包樹。

一群大象讓小王子發噱：

「那我得把大象一隻一隻疊起來才行。」

他聰明地注意到：

「猴麵包樹在長大以前，也是小小的。」

「不錯！可是為什麼你想讓羊去把小猴麵包樹吃掉呢？」

他答道：「唉！這很明顯嘛！」彷彿事實就擺在眼前。可是我卻絞盡腦汁才了解問題所在。

原來，在小王子的星球上有益草也有壞草，就跟其他星球一樣。所以，星球上也會有益草的好種子和壞草的壞種子，可是你看不見種子。

I pointed out to the little prince that baobabs were not little bushes, but, on the contrary, trees as big as castles; and that even if he took a whole herd of elephants away with him, the herd would not eat up one single baobab.

The idea of the herd of elephants made the little prince laugh.

"We would have to put them one on top of the other," he said.

But he made a wise comment:

"Before they grow so big, the baobabs start out by being little."

"That is strictly correct," I said. "But why do you want the sheep to eat the little baobabs?"

He answered me at once, "Oh, come, come!", as if he were speaking of something that was self-evident. And I was obliged to make a great mental effort to solve this problem, without any assistance.

Indeed, as I learned, there were on the planet where the little prince lived—as on all planets—good plants and bad plants. In consequence, there were good seeds from good plants, and bad seeds from bad plants. But seeds are invisible.

種子在泥土裡悄悄地沉睡，直到其中一顆種子悠悠醒轉……

於是它伸展開來，朝向太陽害羞地長出一個可愛漂亮的嫩芽。如果是株蘿蔔苗或是玫瑰花苗，就任由它恣意生長。如果是株壞苗，一發現就應該盡快剷除。

小王子的星球上有些很可怕的種子……那就是猴麵包樹的種子。

這個星球的泥土裡到處藏著猴麵包樹的種子。要是沒有盡早剷除猴麵包樹樹苗，可能就會再也無法擺脫它。猴麵包樹會占據整個星球，而樹根能穿透星球。如果星球很小，猴麵包樹又太多，一顆星球最後的下場將是支離破碎。

「這是自我約束的問題。」後來小王子對我說。

They sleep deep in the heart of the earth's darkness, until some one among them is seized with the desire to awaken.

Then this little seed will stretch itself and begin   timidly at first—to push a charming little sprig inoffensively upward toward the sun. If it is only a sprout of radish or the sprig of a rose-bush, one would let it grow wherever it might wish. But when it is a bad plant, one must destroy it as soon as possible, the very first instant that one recognizes it.

Now there were some terrible seeds on the planet that was the home of the little prince; and these were the seeds of the baobab.

The soil of that planet was infested with them. A baobab is something you will never, never be able to get rid of if you attend to it too late. It spreads over the entire planet. It bores clear through it with its roots. And if the planet is too small, and the baobabs are too many, they split it in pieces...

"It is a question of discipline," the little prince said to me later on.

「早上起床梳洗完畢以後，就要小心翼翼地替整顆星球梳洗。要規定自己定時拔掉猴麵包樹樹苗。這種樹苗和玫瑰花苗非常相似，一旦分辨出是猴麵包樹樹苗，就要拔除。這個工作很無聊，但是很簡單。」

後來有一天，他建議我試著畫一張漂亮的圖，讓我故鄉的孩子們能深深記住這件事。

他對我說：「如果有一天他們出門旅行，這張圖就會派上用場。有時候人會拖延逃避，沒有馬上去做自己的工作，卻也沒出什麼大問題。不過要是碰上猴麵包樹，就會變成一場災難。我曾經到過一個星球上面住了一個懶鬼，他漏了三株樹苗……」

"When you've finished your own toilet in the morning, then it is time to attend to the toilet of your planet, just so, with the greatest care. You must see to it that you pull up regularly all the baobabs, at the very first moment when they can be distinguished from the rosebushes which they resemble so closely in their earliest youth. It is very tedious work," the little prince added, *"but very easy."*

And one day he said to me: "You ought to make a beautiful drawing, so that the children where you live can see exactly how all this is. That would be very useful to them if they were to travel some day. Sometimes." he added, *"there is no harm in putting off a piece of work until another day. But when it is a matter of baobabs, that always means a catastrophe. I knew a planet that was inhabited by a lazy man. He neglected three little bushes…"*

照著小王子的描述，我畫了這個星球。我不太喜歡說教，可是大家幾乎都不明白猴麵包樹有多可怕，而且對那些誤入小行星的人來說，也相當危險。因此這次我放下堅持，決定說教一次：「孩子們，要小心那些猴麵包樹呀！」

我的朋友跟我一樣，長期處在猴麵包樹的危險邊緣，卻不知道它有多危險。為了警告朋友，我花了很多心力畫下這張圖。要是有人能從中學到教訓，我多花些精神也是值得的。

也許你會問，為什麼這本書其他的圖都沒有猴麵包樹這幅壯觀呢？

答案很簡單：我試過，但沒有成功。或許我在畫猴麵包樹的時候，心中相當急切的緣故吧。

So, as the little prince described it to me, I have made a drawing of that planet. I do not much like to take the tone of a moralist. But the danger of the baobabs is so little understood, and such considerable risks would be run by anyone who might get lost on an asteroid, that for once I am breaking through my reserve. "Children," I say plainly, "watch out for the baobabs!"

My friends, like myself, have been skirting this danger for a long time, without ever knowing it; and so it is for them that I have worked so hard over this drawing. The lesson which I pass on by this means is worth all the trouble it has cost me.

Perhaps you will ask me, "Why are there no other drawing in this book as magnificent and impressive as this drawing of the baobabs?"

The reply is simple. I have tried. But with the others I have not been successful. When I made the drawing of the baobabs I was carried beyond myself by the inspiring force of urgent necessity.

6

啊！小王子，我就這麼一點一滴地了解你充滿憂愁的生活。在很長的一段時間裡，你唯一的樂趣就是靜靜看著太陽西下。我在第四天早上才知道這件事。那時你對我說：

「我喜歡看日落。我們去看日落吧！」

「但是要等……」

「等什麼？」

「等太陽西沉。」

Oh, little prince! Bit by bit I came to understand the secrets of your sad little life... For a long time you had found your only entertainment in the quiet pleasure of looking at the sunset. I learned that new detail on the morning of the fourth day, w hen you said to me:

"I am very fond of sunsets. Come, let us go look at a sunset now."

"But we must wait," I said.

"Wait? For what?"

"For the sunset. We must wait until it is time."

剛開始你似乎吃了一驚，隨後你就笑自己糊塗。並對我說：

「我老是以為自己還在家裡！」

大家都知道，在美國的中午艷陽高照的時候，法國卻已經是日暮西山。

只要能在一分鐘以內趕到法國，就可以看到夕陽。可惜法國太過遙遠。但是在你的星球上，只要把椅子往前拉幾步就夠了。任何時候你想看日落都沒問題⋯⋯

「有一天，我看了四十四次日落。」

過一會兒，你又說：

「你明白的⋯⋯每當人非常非常悲傷的時候，就喜歡看日落。」

「看四十四次日落的那一天，你非常非常悲傷？」

小王子沒有回答。

At first you seemed to be very much surprised. And then you laughed to yourself. You said to me:

"I am always thinking that I am at home!"

Just so. Everybody knows that when it is noon in the United States the sun is setting over France.

If you could fly to France in one minute, you could go straight into the sunset, right from noon. Unfortunately, France is too far away for that. But on your tiny planet, my little prince, all you need do is move your chair a few steps. You can see the day end and the twilight falling whenever you like...

"One day," you said to me, "I saw the sunset forty-four times!"

And a little later you added:

"You know—one loves the sunset, when one is so sad..."

"Were you so sad, then?" I asked, "on the day of the forty-four sunsets?"

But the little prince made no reply.

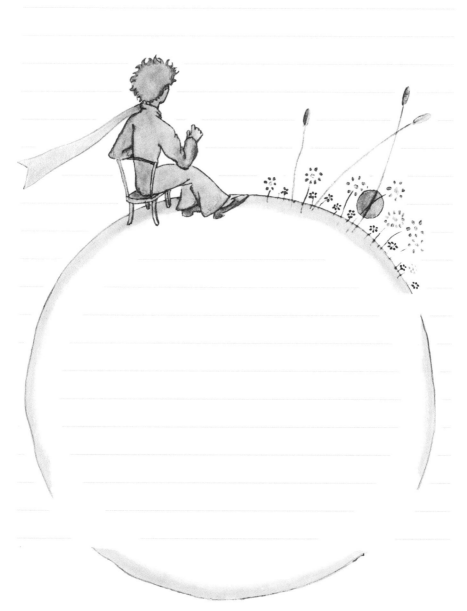

7

第五天，還是同樣託了那隻羊的福，才揭開了小王子的祕密生活。他彷彿經過漫長靜默的思考，突然得到結果一般，沒頭沒尾地問道：

「羊會吃小灌木，那也會吃花嗎？」

「羊碰到什麼就吃什麼。」

「帶刺的花也吃嗎？」

「帶刺的花也吃！」

「那刺有什麼用呀？」

我不知道。那時我正忙著把一顆卡在引擎上的螺絲弄下來。我發現飛機嚴重故障，擔心得不得了。

On the fifth day—again, as always, it was thanks to the sheep—the secret of the little prince's life was revealed to me. Abruptly, without anything to lead up to it, and as if the question had been born of long and silent meditation on his problem, he demanded:

"A sheep—if it eats little bushes, does it eat flowers, too?"

"A sheep," I answered, "eats anything it finds in its reach."

"Even flowers that have thorns?"

"Yes, even flowers that have thorns."

"Then the thorns—what use are they?"

I did not know. At that moment I was very busy trying to unscrew a bolt that had got stuck in my engine. I was very much worried, for it was becoming clear to me that the breakdown of my plane was extremely serious.

身上的飲用水也快見底了，這是我最害怕的狀況。

「那刺有什麼用呀？」

一旦提出問題，小王子就不會放棄。這個該死的螺絲讓我一肚子火，所以就隨便回了一句：

「刺根本沒什麼用，不過是花朵身上邪惡的一部分。」

「哦！」

一陣沉默過後，他埋怨地對我說：

「我不相信！花朵天真弱小，一直在想辦法保護自己，她們相信自己身上的刺很可怕……」

And I had so little drinking-water left that I had to fear for the worst.

"The thorns—what use are they?"

The little prince never let go of a question, once he had asked it. As for me, I was upset over that bolt. And I answered with the first thing that came into my head:

"The thorns are of no use at all. Flowers have thorns just for spite!"

"Oh!"

There was a moment of complete silence. Then the little prince flashed back at me, with a kind of resentfulness:

"I don't believe you! Flowers are weak creatures. They are naive. They reassure themselves as best they can. They believe that their thorns are terrible weapons…"

我沒有回應。那時候我心裡想的是，如果這個螺絲再弄不下來，我就一錘敲了它。

　　小王子打斷了我的思緒，說：

　　「你真的覺得，花……」

　　「不是、不是！我什麼都不覺得！我剛剛是隨便說說的。我現在忙著做重要的事！」

　　他呆呆地盯著我。

　　「重要的事？」

　　他看著我手上拿著錘子，手指沾滿引擎機油，彎腰對著一個他覺得醜陋不堪的東西。

I did not answer. At that instant I was saying to myself: "If this bolt still won't turn, I am going to knock it out with the hammer."

Again the little prince disturbed my thoughts.

"And you actually believe that the flowers—"

"Oh, no!" I cried. "No, no no! I don't believe anything. I answered you with the first thing that came into my head. Don't you see—I am very busy with matters of consequence!"

He stared at me, thunderstruck.

"Matters of consequence!"

He looked at me there, with my hammer in my hand, my fingers black with engine-grease, bending down over an object which seemed to him extremely ugly…

「你的口氣就跟那些大人一樣！」

這話讓我有點尷尬。他又無情地說道：

「你什麼都搞不清楚……你把所有東西都混在一起了！」

小王子真的很生氣。他搖著頭，金髮隨風晃動。

「我曾經去過一個星球，那裡住了一位紅臉先生。他從來沒有聞過一朵花，也沒有看過一顆星星。他誰也不喜歡。除了算數，他沒做過別的事。他跟你一樣，整天只會說：『我有重要的事要忙，我是個認真的人』。他居然還引以為傲。他簡直不是個人，是一個蘑菇！」

「什麼？」

「是一個蘑菇！」

小王子氣得臉色發白。

"You talk just like the grown-ups!"

That made me a little ashamed. But he went on, relentlessly:

"You mix everything up together… You confuse everything…"

He was really very angry. He tossed his golden curls in the breeze.

"I know a planet where there is a certain red-faced gentleman. He has never smelled a flower. He has never looked at a star. He has never loved any one. He has never done anything in his life but add up figures. And all day he says over and over, just like you: 'I am busy with matters of consequence!' And that makes him swell up with pride. But he is not a man—he is a mushroom!"

"A what?"

"A mushroom!"

The little prince was now white with rage.

「幾百萬年以來花身上都長著刺，幾百萬年以來羊也還是在吃花。想知道爲什麼花要用那麼多力氣長刺，結果刺卻沒有什麼用，這難道不算重要的事？難道羊跟花的戰爭不重要？難道不比紅臉先生的帳目重要？

「如果我認識一朵在這世界上獨一無二的花，只長在我的星球上，要是小羊早上一個不注意咬了花一口，這朵花就毀了。哦，你也覺得這不重要！」

他的臉氣得由白轉紅，又接著說：

「如果一個人愛上在億萬顆星星中獨一無二的一朵花，他只要注視這些星星就會感到快樂。

"The flowers have been growing thorns for millions of years. For millions of years the sheep have been eating them just the same. And is it not a matter of consequence to try to understand why the flowers go to so much trouble to grow thorns which are never of any use to them? Is the warfare between the sheep and the flowers not important? Is this not of more consequence than a fat red-faced gentleman's sums?

"And if I know—I, myself—one flower which is unique in the world, which grows nowhere but on my planet, but which one little sheep can destroy in a single bite some morning, without even noticing what he is doing—Oh! You think that is not important!"

His face turned from white to red as he continued:

"If some one loves a flower, of which just one single blossom grows in all the millions and millions of stars, it is enough to make him happy just to look at the stars.

「他會告訴自己：『我的花就在那裡的一顆星星上……』但羊要是吃了這朵花，那一瞬間他眼中每顆星星都將黯淡無光！而你覺得這一點也不重要！」

他一句話也說不出來了，哽咽哭泣。

夜幕早已低垂。我丟下手裡的工具。我把錘子、螺絲、乾渴和死亡全都拋在腦後。在一顆星球上，在我的行星上，在地球上，有一個小王子需要安慰！我抱著他，輕輕晃動說：

「你愛的那朵花沒有生命危險……我會畫一個嘴套給你的小羊……我會畫幾個柵欄給你的花……我會……」

我不知道自己還能說些什麼。我覺得自己很笨拙。我不知道該怎麼做才能碰觸他的內心，或是怎麼做才能再進入他的內心……

太神祕了！這淚水的王國！

"He can say to himself, 'Somewhere, my flower is there…' But if the sheep eats the flower, in one moment all his stars will be darkened… And you think that is not important!"

He could not say anything more. His words were choked by sobbing.

The night had fallen. I had let my tools drop from my hands. Of what moment now was my hammer, my bolt, or thirst, or death? On one star, one planet, my planet, the Earth, there was a little prince to be comforted. I took him in my arms, and rocked him. I said to him:

"The flower that you love is not in danger. I will draw you a muzzle for your sheep. I will draw you a railing to put around your flower. I will—"

I did not know what to say to him. I felt awkward and blundering. I did not know how I could reach him, where I could overtake him and go on hand in hand with him once more.

It is such a secret place, the land of tears.

沒多久我就知道了更多關於這朵花的事。

　在小王子的星球上，一直都長著一些只有單層花瓣、普通的花。這些小花占不了多少地方，也沒有打擾到誰。清晨她們在草叢間綻放，到晚上就靜靜凋謝。

　但是有一天，不知從哪裡來的種子突然抽了新芽。小王子近距離地注視這株與眾不同的新苗：說不定這是新品種的猴麵包樹呢。

I soon learned to know this flower better.

On the little prince's planet the flowers had always been very simple. They had only one ring of petals; they took up no room at all; they were a trouble to nobody. One morning they would appear in the grass, and by night they would have faded peacefully away.

But one day, from a seed blown from no one knew where, a new flower had come up; and the little prince had watched very closely over this small sprout which was not like any other small sprouts on his planet. It might, you see, have been a new kind of baobab.

但是，這株新苗很快就不再長大，而且準備孕育出一朵花。屏弱的幼枝上長了一個很大的花苞，小王子覺得這絕對會開出一朵奇妙的花來。但這朵花卻躲在綠色的房間中，花了很多時間精心打扮。

　　她細細挑選出場時身上的顏色，慢慢地穿上，一片一片調整自己的花瓣。她不想像罌粟花一般皺巴巴地現身，她只想光彩奪目地降臨這世間。是的，她很愛漂亮，所以她神祕的梳妝打扮耗費了許多時日。

　　一天清晨，在太陽剛升起的那一刻，她綻放了。

　　她細膩地做了那麼多事前準備，卻打著哈欠說：

　　「我剛睡醒，頭髮亂糟糟的，讓你見笑了……」

But the shrub soon stopped growing, and began to get ready to produce a flower. The little prince, who was present at the first appearance of a huge bud, felt at once that some sort of miraculous apparition must emerge from it. But the flower was not satisfied to complete the preparations for her beauty in the shelter of her green chamber.

She chose her colours with the greatest care. She adjusted her petals one by one. She did not wish to go out into the world all rumpled, like the field poppies. It was only in the full radiance of her beauty that she wished to appear. Oh, yes! She was a coquettish creature! And her mysterious adornment lasted for days and days.

Then one morning, exactly at sunrise, she suddenly showed herself.

And, after working with all this painstaking precision, she yawned and said:

"Ah! I am scarcely awake. I beg that you will excuse me. My petals are still all disarranged…"

小王子再也無法隱藏自己的愛慕：

「你好漂亮啊！」

「可不是嗎？」花兒輕輕地說：「我是和太陽同時誕生的……」

小王子發現這朵花不太懂得謙虛，可是她太動人了！

她立刻又說：「我想，現在應該是早餐時間了，你那麼善良，應該也替我準備了一些……」

小王子有些困惑，卻還是找來一個澆水壺與滿壺乾淨的清水，灌溉花兒。

But the little prince could not restrain his admiration:

"Oh! How beautiful you are!"

"Am I not?" the flower responded, sweetly. "And I was born at the same moment as the sun…"

The little prince could guess easily enough that she was not any too modest — but how moving — and exciting — she was!

"I think it is time for breakfast," she added an instant later. "If you would have the kindness to think of my needs —"

And the little prince, completely abashed, went to look for a sprinkling-can of fresh water. So, he tended the flower.

於是，這朵花很快就開始用她帶點多疑的虛榮心折磨小王子。比方說有一天，她跟小王子說起她身上的四根刺：

「老虎張牙舞爪地撲過來，我也不怕！」

小王子回了一句：「我這個星球上沒有老虎，而且老虎也不吃草。」

花兒悠悠地說道：「我不是草。」

「對不起。」

「我不怕老虎，可我怕颱風。你沒有替我準備屏風嗎？」

小王子注意到：「怕颱風……這對一株植物來說，真是不幸。這朵花真是複雜難懂……」

「晚上你要替我蓋上玻璃罩。你的星球太冷了，住得不舒服，我來的地方……」

So, too, she began very quickly to torment him with her vanity—which was, if the truth be known, a little difficult to deal with. One day, for instance, when she was speaking of her four thorns, she said to the little prince:

"Let the tigers come with their claws!"

"There are no tigers on my planet," the little prince objected. "And, anyway, tigers do not eat weeds."

"I am not a weed," the flower replied, sweetly.

"Please excuse me…"

"I am not at all afraid of tigers," she went on, "but I have a horror of drafts. I suppose you wouldn't have a screen for me?"

"A horror of drafts—that is bad luck, for a plant," remarked the little prince, and added to himself, "This flower is a very complex creature…"

"At night I want you to put me under a glass globe. It is very cold where you live. In the place I came from—"

她的話突然硬生生斷在這裡。她來的時候是顆種子，根本沒見過別的世界。她對於自己差點說了個天真的謊話，而且還被識破，感覺有些懊惱。她輕咳兩三聲，為了讓小王子覺得愧咎，她說道：

　　「屏風呢？」

　　「我本來要去找，可是你剛剛在跟我說話……」

　　於是花兒用力咳了好一陣子，好把錯怪在小王子頭上。

　　儘管小王子真心誠意地喜歡這朵花，還是立刻對她產生了懷疑。小王子太過認真看待一些不重要的話，反倒讓自己不開心。

But she interrupted herself at that point. She had come in the form of a seed. She could not have known anything of any other worlds. Embarassed over having let herself be caught on the verge of such an untruth , she coughed two or three times, in order to put the little prince in the wrong.

"The screen?"

"I was just going to look for it when you spoke to me…"

Then she forced her cough a little more so that he should suffer from remorse just the same.

So the little prince, in spite of all the good will that was inseparable from his love, had soon come to doubt her. He had taken seriously words which were without importance, and it made him very unhappy.

「我不該聽她的，」有一天他這麼告訴我：

「絕對不要聽信那些花說的話，應該看著她們、聞著她們就夠了。這朵花讓我的星球香氣四溢，可是我卻不知道慶幸。老虎的事讓我動怒，其實我應該要同情她才是⋯⋯」

「我真的是什麼也不懂！我應該用她做的事來判斷這朵花是好是壞，而不是聽她說的那些話。

她讓我的生活充滿芬芳，她點亮了我的生命，我根本不應該離開她跑出來！我應該要猜到，在她可憐差勁的花招背後還隱藏著柔情。

花是一種太矛盾的生物！我那時太稚嫩，還不懂得愛情。」

"I ought not to have listened to her," he confided to me one day.

"One never ought to listen to the flowers. One should simply look at them and breathe their fragrance. Mine perfumed all my planet. But I did not know how to take pleasure in all her grace. This tale of claws, which disturbed me so much, should only have filled my heart with tenderness and pity."

And he continued his confidences:

"The fact is that I did not know how to understand anything! I ought to have judged by deeds and not by words.

She cast her fragrance and her radiance over me. I ought never to have run away from her... I ought to have guessed all the affection that lay behind her poor little strategems.

Flowers are so inconsistent! But I was too young to know how to love her..."

9

　　我想小王子是趁著候鳥遷徙的時候離開的。

　　在出發的那天早上，他把星球整理得井井有條，把星球上的活火山打掃乾淨。小王子有兩座活火山，早上熱早餐的時候很方便。他還有一座死火山，不過他說，說不定它哪天就會爆發呢！所以他也把死火山的通道打掃乾淨，就算死火山復燃，也會緩慢規律地燃燒，而不至於爆發。火山爆發就像煙囪起火。

　　很明顯，我們地球上的人類身材太小所以不能打掃火山，這也是為什麼火山總是給我們帶來各種麻煩。

I believe that for his escape he took advantage of the migration of a flock of wild birds.

On the morning of his departure he put his planet in perfect order. He carefully cleaned out his active volcanoes. He possessed two active volcanoes; and they were very convenient for heating his breakfast in the morning. He also had one volcano that was extinct. But, as he said, "One never knows!" So he cleaned out the extinct volcano, too. If they are well cleaned out, volcanoes burn slowly and steadily, without any eruptions. Volcanic eruptions are like fires in a chimney.

On our earth we are obviously much too small to clean out our volcanoes. That is why they bring no end of trouble upon us.

小王子帶著憂愁，把最後幾株猴麵包樹樹苗連根拔起。他以為自己再也不會回來了。離開的那天早上，這些每天做慣的事卻讓他覺得特別珍貴。他最後一次替花澆水，準備替她蓋上玻璃罩的時候，他發現淚水已經在眼眶中打轉。

　　「再見。」他對花說。

　　不過花並沒有回話。

　　「再見。」他又說了一次。

　　花咳嗽了起來，卻不是因為感冒。

The little prince also pulled up, with a certain sense of dejection, the last little shoots of the baobabs. He believed that he would never want to return. But on this last morning all these familiar tasks seemed very precious to him. And when he watered the flower for the last time, and prepared to place her under the shelter of her glass globe, he realised that he was very close to tears.

"Goodbye," he said to the flower.

But she made no answer.

"Goodbye," he said again.

The flower coughed. But it was not because she had a cold.

她終於開口：「我太愚蠢了。請你原諒我。祝你幸福。」

　　這朵花沒有一句抱怨，小王子大吃了一驚，當場楞住了，手裡的玻璃罩還舉在半空中。小王子不懂她爲什麼如此溫柔平靜。

　　「是的，我愛你。」花兒對他說：「都是我的錯，你才會一點也不知情。這都不重要了。不過，你也和我一樣愚蠢。祝你以後找到幸福。罩子就留在那裡吧，我用不到了。」

"I have been silly," she said to him, at last. "I ask your forgiveness. Try to be happy..."

He was surprised by this absence of reproaches. He stood there all bewildered, the glass globe held arrested in mid-air. He did not understand this quiet sweetness.

"Of course I love you," the flower said to him. "It is my fault that you have not known it all the while. That is of no importance. But you—you have been just as foolish as I. Try to be happy... let the glass globe be. I don't want it any more."

「但要是颱風……」

「我的感冒沒那麼嚴重……夜裡的涼風對我有好處。我畢竟還是朵花。」

「萬一有其他的生物……」

「要是我想認識幾隻蝴蝶，就要受得了身上爬著兩三隻毛毛蟲。聽說蝴蝶很美。你想還會有誰來看我？你馬上就要去很遠很遠的地方了。至於野獸，我一點都不怕，我也有爪子。」

她天真地亮出那四根刺，隨後又說：

「別再依依不捨了，真煩！你既然下定決心要離開，現在就走吧！」

其實她是因為怕小王子看到她哭。真是一朵非常驕傲的花……

"But the wind—"

"My cold is not so bad as all that… the cool night air will do me good. I am a flower."

"But the animals—"

"Well, I must endure the presence of two or three caterpillars if I wish to become acquainted with the butterflies. It seems that they are very beautiful. And if not the butterflies—and the caterpillars—who will call upon me? You will be far away… as for the large animals—I am not at all afraid of any of them. I have my claws."

And, naively, she showed her four thorns. Then she added:

"Don't linger like this. You have decided to go away. Now go!"

For she did not want him to see her crying. She was such a proud flower…

10

　　小王子的星球附近，還有 325、326、327、328、329、330 等幾顆小行星。於是他開始拜訪這幾顆星球，想給自己找點事做，也順道增長見聞。

　　第一顆星球上住了一個國王。國王穿著一身紫色絲綢配上貂皮的大禮服，坐在樣式簡單卻莊嚴的寶座上。

　　他一看到小王子便大喊：「啊！我的良民來了。」

　　小王子心想：「他根本沒見過我，怎麼會認識我呢？」

　　他不知道，這個世界在國王的眼裡相當單純，所有人都是國王的臣民。

　　「上前來，讓我好好看看你。」國王對小王子說。國王非常驕傲，因為他終於是某個人的國王了。

He found himself in the neighborhood of the asteroids 325, 326, 327, 328, 329, and 330. He began, therefore, by visiting them, in order to add to his knowledge.

The first of them was inhabited by a king. Clad in royal purple and ermine, he was seated upon a throne which was at the same time both simple and majestic.

"Ah! Here is a subject," exclaimed the king, when he saw the little prince coming.

And the little prince asked himself:

"How could he recognize me when he had never seen me before?"

He did not know how the world is simplified for kings. To them, all men are subjects.

"Approach, so that I may see you better," said the king, who felt consumingly proud of being at last a king over somebody.

小王子環顧四周，卻不知道該坐在哪裡，因為整個星球都被國王漂亮的貂皮袍襴占據了。他只好站著不動，當他站得累了，就打了一個哈欠。

國王對他說：「在國王面前打哈欠非常失禮。我不准你打哈欠。」

小王子一臉茫然地說道：「我忍不住，我經過漫長的旅程才來到這裡，中間都沒睡呢。」

國王說：「好吧，我命令你打哈欠。我好多年沒看到人打哈欠了，我現在倒是對哈欠有點好奇。來吧，打個哈欠來看看！這是命令。」

「這樣反而讓我緊張起來了……我打不出哈欠了……」小王子滿臉漲紅。

The little prince looked everywhere to find a place to sit down; but the entire planet was crammed and obstructed by the king's magnificent ermine robe. So he remained standing upright, and, since he was tired, he yawned.

"It is contrary to etiquette to yawn in the presence of a king," the monarch said to him. "I forbid you to do so."

"I can't help it. I can't stop myself," replied the little prince, thoroughly embarrassed. "I have come on a long journey, and I have had no sleep..."

"Ah, then," the king said. "I order you to yawn. It is years since I have seen anyone yawning. Yawns, to me, are objects of curiosity. Come, now! Yawn again! It is an order."

"That frightens me... I cannot, any more..." murmured the little prince, now completely abashed.

「哼、哼！」國王答道：「那我……命令你有時候打哈欠，有時候……」

他有點結巴，顯然是不太高興。

因為身為一個國王最基本的就是要維持自己的權威，受到眾人尊敬景仰。他無法忍受自己的命令遭人違抗，他是一個絕對的君王。不過，他是個善良的人，他所有的命令都是合理的。

「如果我命令，」他流利地說：「命令一位將軍變成海鳥，但這位將軍卻無法遵從我的命令，那就不能怪將軍，而是我的錯。」

"Hum! Hum!" replied the king. "Then I—I order you sometimes to yawn and sometimes to—"

He sputtered a little, and seemed vexed.

For what the king fundamentally insisted upon was that his authority should be respected. He tolerated no disobedience. He was an absolute monarch. But, because he was a very good man, he made his orders reasonable.

"If I ordered a general," he would say, by way of example, "if I ordered a general to change himself into a sea bird, and if the general did not obey me, that would not be the fault of the general. It would be my fault."

小王子害羞地問道：「我可以坐下嗎？」

「我命令你坐下。」國王答道，邊莊嚴地撩了一下他的貂皮袍襬。

可是小王子很好奇。這星球那麼小，國王在這裡能夠統治些什麼呢？

他對國王說：「陛下……請允許我提出一個問題……」

國王連忙宣告：「我命令你問。」

「陛下……您到底在統治什麼？」

國王相當簡單地說：「我統治一切。」

「一切？」

國王慎重地用手比劃他的星球和其他的星球，以及所有星星。

小王子說：「全部都是？」

「全部都是。」原來他不只是個絕對的君王，而且還君臨整個宇宙。

"May I sit down?" came now a timid inquiry from the little prince.

"I order you to do so," the king answered him, and majestically gathered in a fold of his ermine mantle.

But the little prince was wondering… The planet was tiny. Over what could this king really rule?

"Sire," he said to him, "I beg that you will excuse my asking you a question—"

"I order you to ask me a question," the king hastened to assure him.

"Sire—over what do you rule?"

"Over everything," said the king, with magnificent simplicity.

"Over everything?"

The king made a gesture, which took in his planet, the other planets, and all the stars.

"Over all that?" asked the little prince.

"Over all that," the king answered.For his rule was not only absolute: it was also universal.

「那星星也都服從您的命令嗎？」

「當然！」國王說：「我一下命令，它們馬上就得服從。我不能忍受毫無紀律。」

這麼大的權力讓小王子不住讚歎。如果擁有這種權力，他就可以在一天裡看到超過四十四次的日落，比如說七十二次，甚至一百次、二百次日落，而且根本不用移動椅子！這讓他想起那顆被他拋棄的小星球，不禁有些難過。他鼓起勇氣向國王提出一個請求：

「我想看日落，請您幫個忙……命令太陽西沉吧……」

國王說：「如果我命令一位將軍像隻蝴蝶，從這朵花飛到那朵花，或是命令他寫一齣悲劇，或是變成海鳥，他要是不執行命令的話，那麼，到底是他的錯還是我的錯？」

「當然是您錯了。」小王子堅定地答道。

"And the stars obey you?"

"Certainly they do," the king said. "They obey instantly. I do not permit insubordination."

Such power was a thing for the little prince to marvel at. If he had been master of such complete authority, he would have been able to watch the sunset, not forty-four times in one day, but seventy-two, or even a hundred, or even two hundred times, with out ever having to move his chair. And because he felt a bit sad as he remembered his little planet which he had forsaken, he plucked up his courage to ask the king a favor:

"I should like to see a sunset... do me that kindness... Order the sun to set..."

"If I ordered a general to fly from one flower to another like a butterfly, or to write a tragic drama, or to change himself into a sea bird, and if the general did not carry out the order that he had received, which one of us would be in the wrong?" the king demanded. "The general, or myself?"

"You," said the little prince firmly.

「完全正確，」國王接著說：「命令百姓做的事應該是他們力所能及的。權威要先建立在合理的基礎上，百姓才能接受。如果我命令老百姓投海，他們一定會群起發動革命。我的命令要先是合理的，才有權利要求別人服從。」

「那我的日落呢？」小王子提醒他。一旦提出問題，小王子就不會放棄。

「你會看到你的日落。我會命令太陽西沉，不過依照我的統治哲學，要等到條件合適的時候。」

小王子問：「要等到什麼時候呢？」

「嗯……」國王在回答之前，先動手翻開一本厚重的日曆，嘴裡慢慢說道：「嗯……應該……應該是……今天晚上七點四十分！到時候你就會看到我的命令生效。」

"Exactly. One much require from each one the duty which each one can perform," the king went on. "Accepted authority rests first of all on reason. If you ordered your people to go and throw themselves into the sea, they would rise up in revolution. I have the right to require obedience because my orders are reasonable."

"Then my sunset?" the little prince reminded him: for he never forgot a question once he had asked it.

"You shall have your sunset. I shall command it. But, according to my science of government, I shall wait until conditions are favorable."

"When will that be?" inquired the little prince.

"Hum! Hum!" replied the king; and before saying anything else he consulted a bulky almanac. "Hum! Hum! That will be about—about—that will be this evening about twenty minutes to eight. And you will see how well I am obeyed."

小王子打了個哈欠。錯過日落雖然很可惜，不過他有些厭倦了，他對國王說：「我在這裡沒什麼好做的了。我要走了。」

　　「別走！」國王才剛因為擁有一個人民正在驕傲得意，他說：「別走！我讓你做大臣。」

　　「什麼大臣？」

　　「司……司法大臣！」

　　「可是這裡沒人可以審判呀。」

　　「這很難說，」國王說：「我還沒有完整巡視過我的王國呢。我年紀大了，這裡又沒地方放出巡的馬車，而且我一走路就累。」

　　「哦！但是我已經看過了。」小王子說，並回頭看看星球的另一面。那裡一個人也沒有……

The little prince yawned. He was regretting his lost sunset. And then, too, he was already beginning to be a little bored. "I have nothing more to do here," he said to the king "So I shall set out on my way again."

"Do not go," said the king, who was very proud of having a subject. "Do not go. I will make you a Minister!"

"Minister of what?"

"Minster of — of Justice!"

"But there is nobody here to judge!"

"We do not know that," the king said to him. "I have not yet made a complete tour of my kingdom. I am very old. There is no room here for a carriage. And it tires me to walk."

"Oh, but I have looked already!" said the little prince, turning around to give one more glance to the other side of the planet. On that side, as on this, there was nobody at all...

「那你可以審判自己呀！」國王回答。「這是世界上頭等的難事。審判自己比審判別人要難得多！你如果能夠正確審判自己，你將成為真正的智者。」

「的確，」小王子說：「但是我在哪裡都可以審判自己，沒有必要住在這個星球上。」

國王說：「嗯……我想在這個星球上藏著一隻上了年紀的老鼠。每到晚上我都能聽見牠的聲音。你可以審判牠，時不時給牠判個死刑。你的判決可以決定牠的生死。不過你要省著點用，每次判完刑就要赦免牠，因為我們只有一隻老鼠。」

"Then you shall judge yourself," the king answered. "that is the most difficult thing of all. It is much more difficult to judge oneself than to judge others. If you succeed in judging yourself rightly, then you are indeed a man of true wisdom."

"Yes," said the little prince, "but I can judge myself anywhere. I do not need to live on this planet.

"Hum! Hum!" said the king. "I have good reason to believe that somewhere on my planet there is an old rat. I hear him at night. You can judge this old rat. From time to time you will condemn him to death. Thus his life will depend on your justice. But you will pardon him on each occasion; for he must be treated thriftily. He is the only one we have."

「我不喜歡判任何人死刑。我想我還是走吧。」小王子回答。

「不行。」國王說。

小王子做好了離開的準備,但他不想見到老國王傷心,說道:

「如果陛下希望一下命令就能立刻被執行,您現在可以合理地命令我。比如說,您可以命令我在一分鐘之內離開這個星球。我想條件已經很合適了……」

國王沒有回答,小王子猶豫了一會兒,然後嘆了口氣,就走了。

「我任命你當我的大使。」國王匆匆忙忙地大聲喊道。

國王擺出一副無上權威的樣子。

「大人都好奇怪。」小王子踏上旅途,邊喃喃自語說。

"I," replied the little prince, "do not like to condemn anyone to death. And now I think I will go on my way."

"No," said the king.

But the little prince, having now completed his preparations for departure, had no wish to grieve the old monarch.

"If Your Majesty wishes to be promptly obeyed," he said, "he should be able to give me a reasonable order. He should be able, for example, to order me to be gone by the end of one minute. It seems to me that conditions are favorable..."

As the king made no answer, the little prince hesitated a moment. Then, with a sigh, he took his leave.

"I made you my Ambassador," the king called out, hastily.

He had a magnificent air of authority.

"The grown-ups are very strange," the little prince said to himself, as he continued on his journey.

11

第二個星球上住了一個愛慕虛榮的人。

「哇！我的仰慕者來了！」虛榮的人一看到小王子，遠遠就大喊了起來。

在虛榮的人眼裡，其他每一個人都是他們的仰慕者。

「你好！」小王子說。「你的帽子好奇怪。」

「這是致意用的。」虛榮的人說：「每當人們為我歡呼的時候，我就用帽子向他們致意。可惜從來沒人路過這裡。」

小王子不懂他的意思，說道：「是嗎？」

虛榮的人提議說：「用你的手去拍另一隻手。」

小王子拍拍手。虛榮的人謙虛地舉起帽子向小王子致意。

The second planet was inhabited by a conceited man.

"Ah! Ah! I am about to receive a visit from an admirer!" he exclaimed from afar, when he first saw the little prince coming.

For, to conceited men, all other men are admirers.

"Good morning," said the little prince. "That is a queer hat you are wearing."

"It is a hat for salutes," the conceited man replied. "It is to raise in salute when people acclaim me. Unfortunately, nobody at all ever passes this way."

"Yes?" said the little prince, who did not understand what the conceited man was talking about.

"Clap your hands, one against the other," the conceited man now directed him.

The little prince clapped his hands. The conceited man raised his hat in a modest salute.

小王子心想：「這次比拜訪國王有趣。」所以他又開始拍手。虛榮的人又舉起帽子向他致意。

小王子持續拍了五分鐘手，就開始厭倦這個單調的遊戲。他說：

「怎麼做才能讓你把帽子脫下來呢？」

虛榮的人根本聽不進他說的話，因為每個愛慕虛榮的人都只聽得見讚美的話語。

他問小王子：「你真的很崇拜我嗎？」

「什麼是『崇拜』？」

"This is more entertaining than the visit to the king," the little prince said to himself. And he began again to clap his hands, one against the other. The conceited man against raised his hat in salute.

After five minutes of this exercise the little prince grew tired of the game's monotony.

"And what should one do to make the hat come down?" he asked.

But the conceited man did not hear him. Conceited people never hear anything but praise.

"Do you really admire me very much?" he demanded of the little prince.

"What does that mean — 'admire'?"

122

「崇拜就是，你覺得我是這個星球上最美麗的人、衣服最漂亮的人、最有錢的人，還有最聰明的人。」

　　「但你是這個星球上唯一的一個人啊！」

　　「讓我快樂吧，繼續崇拜我吧！」

　　小王子聳聳肩膀說：「我崇拜你，可是為什麼你那麼在意？」

　　然後他離開了這顆星球。

　　「大人真的都好奇怪。」小王子踏上旅途，邊喃喃自語說。

"To admire mean that you regard me as the handsomest, the best-dressed, the richest, and the most intelligent man on this planet."

"But you are the only man on your planet!"

"Do me this kindness. Admire me just the same."

"I admire you," said the little prince, shrugging his shoulders slightly, *"but what is there in that to interest you so much?"*

And the little prince went away.

"The grown-ups are certainly very odd," he said to himself, as he continued on his journey.

12

　　小王子拜訪的下一個星球上住了一個酒鬼。這次拜訪十分倉促，卻令小王子非常憂傷。

　　「你在做什麼？」小王子問酒鬼。酒鬼靜靜地坐著，面前有一堆酒瓶，有些瓶子已經空了，有些還是滿的。

　　「我喝酒。」他陰沉地答道。

　　「你為什麼要喝酒？」小王子問。

　　「為了遺忘。」酒鬼回答。

The next planet was inhabited by a tippler. This was a very short visit, but it plunged the little prince into deep dejection.

"What are you doing there?" he said to the tippler, whom he found settled down in silence before a collection of empty bottles and also a collection of full bottles.

"I am drinking," replied the tippler, with a lugubrious air.

"Why are you drinking?" demanded the little prince.

"So that I may forget," replied the tippler.

小王子已經開始可憐眼前的酒鬼了。他問：「你要忘記什麼？」

酒鬼低下頭，坦誠地說：「我想忘記羞恥。」

「你爲什麼羞恥？」小王子問。心裡很想幫他。

「我因爲酗酒而感到羞恥。」酒鬼說完就再也不願意開口了。

小王子充滿困惑地離開。

「大人眞的都非常非常奇怪。」小王子踏上旅途，邊喃喃自語說。

"Forget what?" inquired the little prince, who already was sorry for him.

"Forget that I am ashamed," the tippler confessed, hanging his head.

"Ashamed of what?" insisted the little prince, who wanted to help him.

"Ashamed of drinking!" The tippler brought his speech to an end, and shut himself up in an impregnable silence.

And the little prince went away, puzzled.

"The grown-ups are certainly very, very odd," he said to himself, as he continued on his journey.

第四個星球是一個商人的星球。這個人忙得不能再忙了，小王子抵達的時候，他甚至連頭都沒有抬起來。

「你好，」小王子對他說：「你的香菸熄了。」

「三加二等於五。五加七等於十二。十二加三等於十五。你好。十五加七，二十二。二十二加六，二十八。我沒時間點菸。二十六加五，三十一。哦！一共是五億一百六十二萬二千七百三十一。」

「五億什麼？」

「嗯？你還在啊？五億一百萬……我也搞不清楚什麼是什麼了。我的工作很多……我，我是個認真的人……跟你閒聊我也得不到任何樂趣！二加五等於七……」

The fourth planet belonged to a businessman. This man was so much occupied that he did not even raise his head at the little prince's arrival.

"Good morning," the little prince said to him. "Your cigarette has gone out."

"Three and two make five. Five and seven make twelve. Twelve and three make fifteen. Good morning. Fifteen and seven make twenty-two. Twenty-two and six make twenty-eight. I haven't time to light it again. Twenty-six and five make thirty-one. Phew! Then that makes five-hundred-and-one-million, six-hundred-twenty-two-thousand, seven-hundred-thirty-one."

"Five hundred million what?" asked the little prince.

"Eh? Are you still there? Five-hundred-and-one million—I can't stop… I have so much to do! I am concerned with matters of consequence. I don't amuse myself with balderdash. Two and five make seven…"

「五億一百萬什麼？」小王子再次問道。一旦提出問題，小王子就不會放棄。

商人抬起頭說：「我住在這個星球已經五十四年了，這段期間裡我只被打擾過三次。第一次被打擾是二十二年前，天知道從哪裡來了一隻金龜子。牠發出恐怖的噪音，讓我的一筆帳目出了四個錯。第二次是十一年前，我的風濕病發作，因為我平常缺少運動。我根本沒有閒工夫四處逛。我，我是個認真的人。現在……是第三次！我剛剛說是五億一百萬……」

「上億個什麼？」

這個商人明白今天是不得安寧了，他說道：

「上億個小東西，有時可以在天空中看到的小東西。」

「蒼蠅？」

"Five-hundred-and-one million what?" repeated the little prince, who never in his life had let go of a question once he had asked it.

The businessman raised his head.

"During the fifty-four years that I have inhabited this planet, I have been disturbed only three times. The first time was twenty-two years ago, when some giddy goose fell from goodness knows where. He made the most frightful noise that resounded all over the place, and I made four mistakes in my addition. The second time, eleven years ago, I was disturbed by an attack of rheumatism. I don't get enough exercise. I have no time for loafing. The third time—well, this is it! I was saying, then, five-hundred-and-one millions—"

"Millions of what?"

The businessman suddenly realized that there was no hope of being left in peace until he answered this question.

"Millions of those little objects," he said, "which one sometimes sees in the sky."

"Flies?"

「不是，是閃閃發光的小東西。」

「蜜蜂？」

「不是，是金色的小東西，無所事事的人常看著這些小東西做白日夢。我，我是個認真的人。我沒空做白日夢。」

「啊，是星星？」

「對，就是星星。」

「你要對五億顆星星做什麼？」

「是五億一百六十二萬二千七百三十一顆星星。我，我是個認真的人，我的計算非常精確。」

「你要對這些星星做什麼？」

「我要做什麼？」

「對。」

"Oh, no. Little glittering objects."

"Bees?"

"Oh, no. Little golden objects that set lazy men to idle dreaming. As for me, I am concerned with matters of consequence. There is no time for idle dreaming in my life."

"Ah! You mean the stars?"

"Yes, that's it. The stars."

"And what do you do with five-hundred millions of stars?"

"Five-hundred-and-one million, six-hundred-twenty-two thousand, seven-hundred-thirty-one. I am concerned with matters of consequence: I am accurate."

"And what do you do with these stars?"

"What do I do with them?"

"Yes."

「什麼也不做。我擁有這些星星。」

「你擁有這些星星？」

「是的。」

「可是我才遇到一個國王，他……」

「國王並不擁有什麼，他們是『統治』。這兩者有非常大的不同。」

「你擁有這麼多星星要做什麼？」

「這些星星讓我變成有錢人。」

「變成有錢人要做什麼？」

「如果有人發現新的星星，要有錢才能買下來。」

小王子喃喃自語說：「這個人的邏輯怎麼跟那個酒鬼有點像呀。」

"Nothing. I own them."

"You own the stars?"

"Yes."

"But I have already seen a king who —"

"Kings do not own, they reign over. It is a very different matter."

"And what good does it do you to own the stars?"

"It does me the good of making me rich."

"And what good does it do you to be rich?"

"It makes it possible for me to buy more stars, if any are ever discovered."

"This man," the little prince said to himself, *"reasons a little like my poor tippler…"*

然而，小王子還有一些疑問：

　　「一個人怎麼可能擁有星星呢？」

　　「那這些星星是誰的？」商人暴躁地反駁小王子。

　　「我不知道，星星不是任何人的。」

　　「那這些星星就是我的，因為我第一個想到要擁有這些星星。」

　　「你先想到就可以嗎？」

　　「當然。當你發現一顆不屬於任何人的鑽石，那這顆鑽石就是你的。當你發現一個無主的小島，那這個小島就是屬於你的。當你想到一個沒人想過的點子，你可以申請專利，那這個點子就是完全屬於你的。既然沒有任何人比我先想到要占有這些星星，那這些星星就是屬於我的。」

　　「你說的也有道理。但是你要對這些星星做什麼？」小王子說。

Nevertheless, he still had some more questions.

"How is it possible for one to own the stars?"

"To whom do they belong?" the businessman retorted, peevishly.

"I don't know. To nobody."

"Then they belong to me, because I was the first person to think of it."

"Is that all that is necessary?"

"Certainly. When you find a diamond that belongs to nobody, it is yours. When you discover an island that belongs to nobody, it is yours. When you get an idea before any one else, you take out a patent on it: it is yours. So with me: I own the stars, because nobody else before me ever thought of owning them."

"Yes, that is true," said the little prince. "And what do you do with them?"

「我管理這些星星。我一遍又一遍數著這些星星。」商人說：「這是一件困難的事情。但我是一個認真的人！」

小王子還是不滿足，他說：

「在我看來，如果我擁有一條圍巾，我會用圍巾圍住我的脖子，隨身帶著它。我要是擁有一朵花，我會摘下我的花，帶著它跟我一起走。可是你卻不能摘下這些星星啊！」

「我摘不下來，但是我可以把星星存在銀行裡。」

「那是什麼意思？」

「意思是說，我把我擁有的星星數目寫在一張小紙片上，然後再把這張小紙片鎖在一個抽屜裡。」

「就這樣？」

「這樣就夠了。」

"I administer them," replied the businessman. *"I count them and recount them. It is difficult. But I am a man who is naturally interested in matters of consequence."*

The little prince was still not satisfied.

"If I owned a silk scarf," he said, *"I could put it around my neck and take it away with me. If I owned a flower, I could pluck that flower and take it away with me. But you cannot pluck the stars from heaven…"*

"No. But I can put them in the bank."

"Whatever does that mean?"

"That means that I write the number of my stars on a little paper. And then I put this paper in a drawer and lock it with a key."

"And that is all?"

"That is enough," said the businessman.

「眞有趣，」小王子心想：「眞夠詩意的，不過這算不上是什麼重要的事。」

對於什麼事是重要的，小王子的想法跟大人的想法非常非常不一樣。

他又說：「我擁有一朵花，每天我都會替她澆水。我還擁有三座火山，每個星期我都會把三座火山全部清理一遍。死火山我也同樣清理，誰曉得它哪天會復活。我擁有火山和花，我對火山有用處，我對花也有用處。但是你對星星一點用處也沒有……」

商人張大了嘴巴卻說不出一句話。然後小王子就離開了。

「大人絕對都是些非比尋常的怪人。」小王子踏上旅途，邊喃喃自語說。

"It is entertaining," thought the little prince. "It is rather poetic. But it is of no great consequence."

On matters of consequence, the little prince had ideas which were very different from those of the grown-ups.

"I myself own a flower," he continued his conversation with the businessman, "which I water every day. I own three volcanoes, which I clean out every week (for I also clean out the one that is extinct; one never knows). It is of some use to my volcanoes, and it is of some use to my flower, that I own them. But you are of no use to the stars…"

The businessman opened his mouth, but he found nothing to say in answer. And the little prince went away.

"The grown-ups are certainly altogether extraordinary," he said simply, talking to himself as he continued on his journey.

14

第五顆星球十分奇怪，在這些星星中它是最小的一顆。

星球上剛好可以容納一盞路燈和一個點燈的人。小王子怎麼也想不出一個合理的解釋，這顆星星藏在天空的角落裡，上頭沒有房舍也沒有居民，那麼這盞路燈和點燈的人到底有什麼用處。

不過他心裡是這麼想的：

「或許點燈的人有些可笑。但是他比起國王、比起愛慕虛榮的人，比起商人跟酒鬼，都更好一點，至少他的工作還算有意義。當他點亮路燈的時候，彷彿他在這個世界上添了一顆星星或一朵花。當他熄滅路燈的時候，好像他讓星星或花朵入睡了一樣。點燈人這個職業很美好，這份美好本身就是一種用處。」

The fifth planet was very strange. It was the smallest of all.

There was just enough room on it for a street lamp and a lamplighter. The little prince was not able to reach any explanation of the use of a street lamp and a lamplighter, somewhere in the heavens, on a planet which had no people, and not one house.

But he said to himself, nevertheless:

"It may well be that this man is absurd. But he is not so absurd as the king, the conceited man, the businessman, and the tippler. For at least his work has some meaning. When he lights his street lamp, it is as if he brought one more star to life, or one flower. When he puts out his lamp, he sends the flower, or the star, to sleep. That is a beautiful occupation. And since it is beautiful, it is truly useful."

小王子一登上這個星球，就滿懷尊敬地向點燈人問好：

「早安。為什麼你把路燈熄了？」

「早安。這是命令。」點燈人答道。

「命令是什麼？」

「就是熄滅路燈。晚安。」

然後他又點亮路燈。

「為什麼你又把路燈點亮了？」

「這是命令。」點燈人答道。

「我不懂。」小王子說。

「沒什麼好懂的。」點燈人說：「命令就是命令。早安。」

他又熄了路燈。

然後他拿出紅色格子手帕，擦擦額頭上的汗。

When he arrived on the planet he respectfully saluted the lamplighter.

"Good morning. Why have you just put out your lamp?"

"Those are the orders," replied the lamplighter. "Good morning."

"What are the orders?"

"The orders are that I put out my lamp. Good evening."

And he lighted his lamp again.

"But why have you just lighted it again?"

"Those are the orders," replied the lamplighter.

"I do not understand," said the little prince.

"There is nothing to understand," said the lamplighter. "Orders are orders. Good morning."

And he put out his lamp.

Then he mopped his forehead with a handkerchief decorated with red squares.

「我的工作真是累死人了。以前還算合理，早上熄燈，晚上再點亮。白天多出來的時間，我可以休息放鬆，晚上多出來的時間我就拿來睡覺……」

「後來命令改變了嗎？」

點燈人說：「命令還是一樣，這才是最悲哀的地方！這個星球一年轉得比一年快，但命令卻從來沒有改過。」

「結果呢？」小王子問道。

「結果現在這個星球每分鐘就轉一圈，我一秒鐘都停不下來。每一分鐘我都要點一次燈，還要滅一次燈！」

「真好玩！你住的地方居然一天只有一分鐘！」

「根本不好玩！」點燈人說：「就在我們聊天的時候，已經過了一個月。」

"I follow a terrible profession. In the old days it was reasonable. I put the lamp out in the morning, and in the evening I lighted it again. I had the rest of the day for relaxation and the rest of the night for sleep."

"And the orders have been changed since that time?"

"The orders have not been changed," said the lamplighter. "That is the tragedy! From year to year the planet has turned more rapidly and the orders have not been changed!"

"Then what?" asked the little prince.

"Then—the planet now makes a complete turn every minute, and I no longer have a single second for repose. Once every minute I have to light my lamp and put it out!"

"That is very funny! A day lasts only one minute, here where you live!"

"It is not funny at all!" said the lamplighter. "While we have been talking together a month has gone by."

「一個月？」

「對。三十分鐘就是三十天！晚安。」

然後他又點亮了路燈。

小王子看著點燈人，他很喜歡這位盡忠職守的點燈人。他想起自己以前為了追逐日落而拉著椅子往前移動的事情。他很想幫助這位新朋友。

「跟你說，」小王子說：「我知道一個方法，讓你想休息的時候就可以休息。」

「我無時無刻都想休息。」點燈人說。

原來一個人可以同時擁有盡忠職守和懶惰兩種特質。

"A month?"

"Yes, a month. Thirty minutes. Thirty days. Good evening."

And he lighted his lamp again.

As the little prince watched him, he felt that he loved this lamplighter who was so faithful to his orders. He remembered the sunsets which he himself had gone to seek, in other days, merely by pulling up his chair; and he wanted to help his friend.

"You know," he said, "I can tell you a way you can rest whenever you want to..."

"I always want to rest," said the lamplighter.

For it is possible for a man to be faithful and lazy at the same time.

小王子繼續說明：

「你的星球那麼小，走三步就可以環球一圈。你只要慢慢走，就可以一直待在太陽光底下。你想休息的時候，就照這樣走……那你希望白天有多長就有多長。」

「這個方法幫不上我什麼忙，我這輩子最喜歡的就是睡覺。」點燈人說。

「眞是不幸。」小王子說。

「眞是不幸。」點燈人說：「早安。」

然後他又滅了路燈。

The little prince went on with his explanation:

"Your planet is so small that three strides will take you all the way around it. To be always in the sunshine, you need only walk along rather slowly. When you want to rest, you will walk—and the day will last as long as you like."

"That doesn't do me much good," said the lamplighter. "The one thing I love in life is to sleep."

"Then you're unlucky," said the little prince.

"I am unlucky," said the lamplighter. "Good morning."

And he put out his lamp.

小王子踏上旅途，邊喃喃自語說：

「像國王、愛慕虛榮的人、酒鬼、商人，這些人一定會瞧不起這位點燈人。可是對我來說，在這群人裡，只有他不會讓我覺得荒謬可笑。或許是因為除了他自己，他還關心一些其他的事。」

他憐憫地嘆了口氣，又自言自語道：

「原本在這群人當中，點燈人是唯一一個可以和我成為朋友的人。可是他的星球真的太小了，容不下兩個人⋯⋯」

不過小王子沒敢承認的是：他最捨不得離開這個美妙星球的原因在於，在那裡每二十四小時就有一千四百四十次日落！

"That man," said the little prince to himself, as he continued farther on his journey, "that man would be scorned by all the others: by the king, by the conceited man, by the tippler, by the businessman. Nevertheless he is the only one of them all who does not seem to me ridiculous. Perhaps that is because he is thinking of something else besides himself."

He breathed a sigh of regret, and said to himself, again:

"That man is the only one of them all whom I could have made my friend. But his planet is indeed too small. There is no room on it for two people..."

What the little prince did not dare confess was that he was sorry most of all to leave this planet, because it was blest every day with one thousand, four hundred and forty sunsets!

15

第六顆星球比前一個星球大了十倍。這裡住著一位老先生，他正埋首寫書。

「啊！探險者來了。」老先生一看到小王子就大喊。

小王子坐在書桌旁邊，微微喘氣。他經歷了那麼多旅程，多麼漫長啊！

「你是從哪裡來的？」老先生問。

「這本這麼厚的是什麼書？你在這裡做什麼？」小王子問。

「我是個地理學家。」老先生回答。

The sixth planet was ten times larger than the last one. It was inhabited by an old gentleman who wrote voluminous books.

"Oh, look! Here is an explorer!" he exclaimed to himself when he saw the little prince coming.

The little prince sat down on the table and panted a little. He had already traveled so much and so far!

"Where do you come from?" the old gentleman said to him.

"What is that big book?" said the little prince. "What are you doing?"

"I am a geographer," the old gentleman said to him.

「什麼是地理學家？」

「地理學家是學者的一種，他知道海洋、河流、城市、山脈、沙漠這些地方的位置在哪裡。」

「真有趣。」小王子說：「我終於碰到擁有一份真正的職業的人了。」他放眼環顧這位地理學家的星球。這是小王子一路上看過最雄偉最壯觀的星球了。

「你的星球好美。這裡有海洋嗎？」

「我不知道。」地理學家說。

「哦！」小王子很失望。「那有山嗎？」

「我不知道。」地理學家說。

「那這裡有城市、河流或沙漠嗎？」

「我也不知道。」地理學家說。

"What is a geographer?" asked the little prince.

"A geographer is a scholar who knows the location of all the seas, rivers, towns, mountains, and deserts."

"That is very interesting," said the little prince. "Here at last is a man who has a real profession!" And he cast a look around him at the planet of the geographer. It was the most magnificent and stately planet that he had ever seen.

"Your planet is very beautiful," he said. "Has it any oceans?"

"I couldn't tell you," said the geographer.

"Ah!" The little prince was disappointed. "Has it any mountains?"

"I couldn't tell you," said the geographer.

"And towns, and rivers, and deserts?"

"I couldn't tell you that, either."

「你不是個地理學家嗎？」

「沒錯，」地理學家說：「但我不是探險者。這個星球一個探險者也沒有。出門去數這裡有多少城市、河流、山脈、海洋、沙漠並不是地理學家的工作。地理學家太重要了，不能出門四處跑。他不能離開辦公室，不過他可以接見探險者。他向探險者提出種種問題，記錄他們的所見所聞。要是他對哪個探險者的經歷感興趣，那地理學家就得著手調查這個探險者的人格品性。」

「爲什麼？」

「因爲對地理學家寫的書來說，說謊的探險者會是一場災難。一個喝酒喝得太多的探險者同樣也是災難。」

"But you are a geographer!"

"Exactly," the geographer said. "But I am not an explorer. I haven't a single explorer on my planet. It is not the geographer who goes out to count the towns, the rivers, the mountains, the seas, the oceans, and the deserts. The geographer is much too important to go loafing about. He does not leave his desk. But he receives the explorers in his study. He asks them questions, and he notes down what they recall of their travels. And if the recollections of any one among them seem interesting to him, the geographer orders an inquiry into that explorer's moral character."

"Why is that?"

"Because an explorer who told lies would bring disaster on the books of the geographer. So would an explorer who drank too much."

「爲什麼？」小王子問。

「人喝醉酒之後看什麼東西都會變成兩個，然後地理學家就會把一座山寫成兩座山。」

「我認識一個人，讓他來當探險者的話一定很糟糕。」小王子說。

「很有可能。如果探險者人品還不錯的話，就要審查他的發現。」

「去實地看看？」

「不，這樣太複雜了，要求探險者拿出證據就好。比如說，他發現了一座大山，就叫他帶些大石頭來。」

地理學家突然激動了起來。

「你，你不就是從遠方來的嗎？你就是一個探險者！快說說你的星球是什麼樣子吧！」

"Why is that?" asked the little prince.

"Because intoxicated men see double. Then the geographer would note down two mountains in a place where there was only one."

"I know some one," said the little prince, "who would make a bad explorer."

"That is possible. Then, when the moral character of the explorer is shown to be good, an inquiry is ordered into his discovery."

"One goes to see it?"

"No. That would be too complicated. But one requires the explorer to furnish proofs. For example, if the discovery in question is that of a large mountain, one requires that large stones be brought back from it."

The geographer was suddenly stirred to excitement.

"But you—you come from far away! You are an explorer! You shall describe your planet to me!"

說完地理學家就打開那本厚重的記事簿，還削了鉛筆。他會先用鉛筆把探險者的描述記下來，等到探險者拿出證據之後，再用鋼筆寫下來。

　　「我們開始吧？」地理學家問。

　　「哦！我住的地方，」小王子說：「沒什麼有趣的，那裡什麼都很小。我有三座火山，其中兩座是活火山，另一座是死火山，不過很難講。」

　　「很難講。」地理學家說。

　　「我還有一朵花。」

　　「我們不記錄花。」地理學家說。

　　「爲什麼？這朵花是我的星球上最美麗的東西。」

　　「因爲花是短暫的。」

　　And, having opened his big register, the geographer sharpened his pencil. The recitals of explorers are put down first in pencil. One waits until the explorer has furnished proofs, before putting them down in ink.

　　"Well?" said the geographer expectantly.

　　"Oh, where I live," said the little prince, "it is not very interesting. It is all so small. I have three volcanoes. Two volcanoes are active and the other is extinct. But one never knows."

　　"One never knows," said the geographer.

　　"I have also a flower."

　　"We do not record flowers," said the geographer.

　　"Why is that? The flower is the most beautiful thing on my planet!"

　　"We do not record them," said the geographer, "because they are ephemeral."

「什麼是『短暫』？」

「地理學叢書是所有的書裡頭是最嚴肅的。」地理學家說：「這種書永遠不會過時。山所在的位置幾乎不會改變，海洋也幾乎不會乾枯。我們記錄的是永恆。」

「可是死火山也有可能會再次爆發。」小王子插嘴道：「什麼是『短暫』？」

「死火山也好，活火山也好，對我們來說都是一樣的。」地理學家說：「真正重要的是山。山是不會換地方的。」

「但是，『短暫』是什麼意思？」小王子第三次問。一旦提出問題，他就不會放棄。

「意思是，有稍縱即逝的危險。」

"What does that mean—'ephemeral'?"

"Geographies," said the geographer, "are the books which, of all books, are most concerned with matters of consequence. They never become old-fashioned. It is very rarely that a mountain changes its position. It is very rarely that an ocean empties itself of its waters. We write of eternal things."

"But extinct volcanoes may come to life again," the little prince interrupted. "What does that mean—'ephemeral'?"

"Whether volcanoes are extinct or alive, it comes to the same thing for us," said the geographer. "The thing that matters to us is the mountain. It does not change."

"But what does that mean—'ephemeral'?" repeated the little prince, who never in his life had let go of a question, once he had asked it.

"It means, 'which is in danger of speedy disappearance.'"

「我的花是稍縱即逝的嗎？」

「當然是。」

小王子自言自語說：「我的花是短暫的，而且她只有四根刺可以保護自己！我居然還讓她孤單地留在我的星球上！」

這是他第一次感到後悔，但他再次鼓起勇氣：

「你可以建議我下一站該去哪裡嗎？」小王子問。

「地球，」地理學家答道：「這個星球頗得讚譽……」

小王子踏上旅途，邊想著他的那朵花。

"Is my flower in danger of speedy disappearance?"

"Certainly it is."

"My flower is ephemeral," the little prince said to himself, *"and she has only four thorns to defend herself against the world. And I have left her on my planet, all alone!"*

That was his first moment of regret. But he took courage once more.

"What place would you advise me to visit now?" he asked.

"The planet Earth," replied the geographer. *"It has a good reputation."*

And the little prince went away, thinking of his flower.

16

第七個星球就是地球。

地球不只是一顆普通的星球！

這裡有一百一十一個國王（當然，沒少算黑人國王）、七千個地理學家、九十萬個商人、七百五十萬個酒鬼、三億一千一百萬個愛慕虛榮的人，也就是說，地球上大約有二十億個大人。

爲了讓你對地球到底多大稍微有個概念，我要告訴你在發現電力之前，在地球的六大洲上想要點亮路燈，需要一支高達四十六萬二千五百一十一人的點燈大軍。

So then the seventh planet was the Earth.

The Earth is not just an ordinary planet!

One can count, there ,one hundred and eleven kings (not forgetting, to be sure, the Negro kings among them), seven thousand geographers, nine hundred thousand businessmen, seven and a half million tipplers, three hundred and eleven million conceited men — that is to say, about two billion grown-ups.

To give you an idea of the size of the Earth, I will tell you that before the invention of electricity it was necessary to maintain, over the whole of the six continents, a veritable army of four hundred and sixty-two thousand, five hundred and eleven lamplighters for the street lamps.

從距離地球稍遠的地方看上去，這個景象相當壯觀。這支點燈大軍的動作猶如芭蕾舞一般有條不紊。

最先上場的是紐西蘭和澳大利亞的點燈人，他們點亮路燈之後，就下場睡覺去了。

再來是中國和西伯利亞的點燈人步上舞臺，隨後也悄悄下台。接著輪到俄羅斯和印度的點燈人。然後是非洲和歐洲的點燈人、南美的點燈人，再來是北美的點燈人。

他們從來不會弄錯上場的順序。真是厲害。

北極只有一盞路燈和一位負責點燈的人，南極也是一樣。地球上唯獨這兩位點燈人不必辛苦勤勞地工作：因為他們每年只要點兩次燈。

Seen from a slight distance, that would make a splendid spectacle. The movements of this army would be regulated like those of the ballet in the opera.

First would come the turn of the lamplighters of New Zealand and Australia. Having set their lamps alight, these would go off to sleep.

Next, the lamplighters of China and Siberia would enter for their steps in the dance, and then they too would be waved back into the wings. After that would come the turn of the lamplighters of Russia and the Indies; then those of Africa and Europe, then those of South America; then those of South America; then those of North America.

And never would they make a mistake in the order of their entry upon the stage. It would be magnificent.

Only the man who was in charge of the single lamp at the North Pole, and his colleague who was responsible for the single lamp at the South Pole—only these two would live free from toil and care: they would be busy twice a year.

17

　當人想表現得俏皮點的時候，說出來的話可能就會跟事實有點脫軌。我在講點燈人的故事時，並不是那麼忠於真實情況，可能會讓不了解這個星球的人有些誤會。

　在地球上，人類占的空間非常少。如果地球上的二十億個人全都站著，而且彷彿開一個集體大會般聚在一起，那只要一個長寬各二十英里的廣場就能輕易容納所有人。太平洋最小的小島就能裝得下全人類。

　當然，大人是不會相信的。

　他們想像自己占據的空間很大，把自己看得像猴麵包樹那麼重要。你可以建議他們動手算算看。大人喜歡數字，這個建議會讓他們很開心。不過別浪費你自己的時間去計算。這根本沒有用處。你可以放心相信我。

When one wishes to play the wit, he sometimes wanders a little from the truth. I have not been altogether honest in what I have told you about the lamplighters. And I realize that I run the risk of giving a false idea of our planet to those who do not know it.

Men occupy a very small place upon the Earth. If the two billion inhabitants who people its surface were all to stand upright and somewhat crowded together, as they do for some big public assembly, they could easily be put into one public square twenty miles long and twenty miles wide. All humanity could be piled up on a small Pacific islet.

The grown-ups, to be sure, will not believe you when you tell them that.

They imagine that they fill a great deal of space. They fancy themselves as important as the baobabs. You should advise them, then, to make their own calculations. They adore figures, and that will please them. But do not waste your time on this extra task. It is unnecessary. You have, I know, confidence in me.

小王子抵達地球的時候，他很訝異這裡連個人影也沒有。他開始擔心自己跑錯了星球。這個時候，在沙漠裡有個閃耀著月色的圓環在移動。

　　小王子謹慎小心地說：「晚安。」

　　「晚安。」蛇說。

　　「我來到的是什麼星球？」小王子問。

　　「這是地球，這裡是非洲。」蛇答道。

　　「啊！……地球上沒有人嗎？」

　　「這裡是沙漠，沒人會待在沙漠裡。地球很大。」蛇說。

When the little prince arrived on the Earth, he was very much surprised not to see any people. He was beginning to be afraid he had come to the wrong planet, when a coil of gold, the color of the moonlight, flashed across the sand.

"Good evening," said the little prince courteously.

"Good evening," said the snake.

"What planet is this on which I have come down?" asked the little prince.

"This is the Earth; this is Africa," the snake answered.

"Ah! Then there are no people on the Earth?"

"This is the desert. There are no people in the desert. The Earth is large," said the snake.

小王子坐在一塊石頭上，抬頭望著天空，他說：

「我真好奇這些星星之所以閃閃發光，是不是為了讓我們有一天能再次找到自己的星球。你看，那是我的星星，剛好在我們正上方……不過，它離我是多麼遠吶！」

「這顆星很美。」蛇說：「你為什麼到這裡來？」

「我跟一朵花吵架了。」小王子說。

「啊！」蛇說。

他們都沉默不語。

「人類在哪裡？」最後是小王子開了口。「在沙漠裡，感覺有點孤獨……」

「在人群當中也一樣會孤獨。」蛇說。

小王子盯著蛇看了很久。

The little prince sat down on a stone, and raised his eyes toward the sky.

"I wonder," he said, "whether the stars are set alight in heaven so that one day each one of us may find his own again… Look at my planet. It is right there above us. But how far away it is!"

"It is beautiful," the snake said. "What has brought you here?"

"I have been having some trouble with a flower," said the little prince.

"Ah!" said the snake.

And they were both silent.

"Where are the men?" the little prince at last took up the conversation again. "It is a little lonely in the desert…"

"It is also lonely among men," the snake said.

The little prince gazed at him for a long time.

「你眞是個怪異的生物，只有手指頭那樣細……」小王子終於說道。

　　「但是我的力量比國王的一根手指頭更強大。」蛇說。

　　小王子露出一個微笑：

　　「你沒那麼強大……你連腳都沒有……連去旅行都不行……」

　　「我可以帶你去很遠很遠的地方，比任何船隻航行得更遠。」蛇說。

　　蛇在小王子的腳踝上繞了一圈，好像一個金色的鐲子。

　　「凡是被我碰上的人，不管是從哪裡來的都會被我送回老家。」蛇又說：「但是你天眞單純，而且還是從另一個星球來的……」

　　小王子沒有回話。

"You are a funny animal," he said at last. "You are no thicker than a finger…"

"But I am more powerful than the finger of a king," said the snake.

The little prince smiled.

"You are not very powerful. You haven't even any feet. You cannot even travel…"

"I can carry you farther than any ship could take you," said the snake.

He twined himself around the little prince's ankle, like a golden bracelet.

"Whomever I touch, I send back to the earth from whence he came," the snake spoke again. "But you are innocent and true, and you come from a star…"

The little prince made no reply.

「我爲你感到難過。在這個花崗石組成的地球上，你是那麼孱弱。如果有一天你太過思念你的星球，我可以幫你。我可以……」

　　「哦！我懂，我很懂。」小王子說：「不過爲什麼你說的話總是像謎語似的？」

　　「這些謎語我都會解開。」蛇說。

　　於是他們再次沉默不語。

"You move me to pity—you are so weak on this Earth made of granite," the snake said. "I can help you, some day, if you grow too homesick for your own planet. I can—"

"Oh! I understand you very well," said the little prince. "But why do you always speak in riddles?"

"I solve them all," said the snake.

And they were both silent.

18

小王子穿越沙漠。這段期間他只碰到了一朵花。一朵不起眼的三瓣花……

「你好。」小王子說。

「你好。」花說。

「人類在哪裡呢？」小王子禮貌地問。

有一次，這朵花曾看到一支駱駝商隊經過。

「人類？我想應該有六、七個人還活著吧。幾年前，我還看過他們。不過，誰都不知道要去哪裡找他們。風會把他們吹跑。他們沒有根，這讓他們的生活很辛苦。」

「再見。」小王子說。

「再見。」花說。

The little prince crossed the desert and met with only one flower. It was a flower with three petals, a flower of no account at all.

"Good morning," said the little prince.

"Good morning," said the flower.

"Where are the men?" the little prince asked, politely.

The flower had once seen a caravan passing.

"Men?" she echoed. "I think there are six or seven of them in existence. I saw them, several years ago. But one never knows where to find them. The wind blows them away. They have no roots, and that makes their life very difficult."

"Goodbye," said the little prince.

"Goodbye," said the flower.

19

後來，小王子爬上一座高山。他以前知道的山，只有家裡那三座只到他膝蓋高的火山。他還曾經把死火山拿來當小凳子。

小王子喃喃自語說：「從這麼高的山上，我應該可以一眼看到整個星球，還有每一個人……」

不過除了尖銳鋒利的懸崖峭壁，其他什麼都看不到。

「你好。」小王子謹慎地開口。

「你好……你好……你好……」回音答道。

「你是誰？」小王子問。「你是誰……你是誰……你是誰……」回音答道。

After that, the little prince climbed a high mountain. The only mountains he had ever known were the three volcanoes, which came up to his knees.

And he used the extinct volcano as a footstool. "From a mountain as high as this one," he said to himself, "I shall be able to see the whole planet at one glance, and all the people…"

But he saw nothing, save peaks of rock that were sharpened like needles.

"Good morning," he said courteously.

"Good morning—Good morning—Good morning," answered the echo.

"Who are you?" said the little prince.

"Who are you—Who are you—Who are you?" answered the echo.

「請你當我的朋友吧，我好孤單。」他說。

「我好孤單……我好孤單……我好孤單……」回音答著。

小王子心想：「這顆星球太奇怪了！到處都那麼乾、那麼尖銳，還那麼鹹。這裡的人根本沒有想像力。他們只會重複每一句別人說的話……在我的星球上，我有一朵花。她總是先開口說話……」

"Be my friends. I am all alone," he said.

"I am all alone — all alone — all alone," answered the echo.

"What a queer planet!" he thought. "It is altogether dry, and altogether pointed, and altogether harsh and forbidding. And the people have no imagination. They repeat whatever one says to them... On my planet I had a flower; she always was the first to speak..."

20

在小王子漫長地走過沙漠、岩石和雪地之後，他終於找到一條道路。而所有的道路都通向人類居住的地方。

「你好。」小王子說。

這是一個玫瑰花園。

「你好。」玫瑰花說道。

小王子望著這些花，全都長得和他的那朵花一模一樣。

「你們是？」小王子驚訝地問。

「我們是玫瑰花。」玫瑰花說。

But it happened that after walking for a long time through sand, and rocks, and snow, the little prince at last came upon a road. And all roads lead to the abodes of men.

"Good morning," he said.

He was standing before a garden, all a-bloom with roses

"Good morning," said the roses.

The little prince gazed at them. They all looked like his flower.

"Who are you?" he demanded, thunderstruck.

"We are roses," the roses said.

「啊！」小王子叫道。

他覺得很難過。那朵花曾經告訴他，她是全宇宙中獨一無二的一朵花。但光是在這座花園裡，就有五千朵跟她一模一樣的花！

「如果她看到這裡的花，」小王子自言自語說：「她一定會非常生氣……她會咳嗽咳得非常用力。爲了不被恥笑，她會假裝自己快死了。

「而我還要假裝去拯救她的生命。如果我不這麼做的話，她爲了讓我也覺得歉疚，可能會眞的去死……」

Ah! said the prince.

And he was overcome with sadness. His flower had told him that she was the only one of her kind in all the universe. And here were five thousand of them, all alike, in one single garden!

"She would be very much annoyed," he said to himself, "if she should see that... she would cough most dreadfully, and she would pretend that she was dying, to avoid being laughed at.

"And I should be obliged to pretend that I was nursing her back to life—for if I did not do that, to humble myself also, she would really allow herself to die..."

他繼續說：「我以為自己很富足，畢竟擁有了一朵獨一無二的花。可惜我擁有的不過是一朵再普通不過的花。一朵普通的花，加上三座只到我膝蓋高的火山，而且其中一座可能永遠不會再活動了……這一切都不會讓我成為一個偉大的王子……」

於是，他伏在草叢間低聲哭泣。

Then he went on with his reflections: "I thought that I was rich, with a flower that was unique in all the world; and all I had was a common rose. A common rose, and three volcanoes that come up to my knees—and one of them perhaps extinct forever… that doesn't make me a very great prince…"

And he lay down in the grass and cried.

21

狐狸就是在這個時候出現的。

「你好。」狐狸說。

「你好。」小王子彬彬有禮地回答。他翻過身,但是什麼也沒看到。

「我在這裡,」那個聲音說:「在蘋果樹下。」

「你是誰?」小王子問了一句,又說:「你很可愛。」

「我是狐狸。」狐狸說。

「過來跟我一起玩吧,」小王子提議說。「我很不開心……」

It was then that the fox appeared.

"Good morning," said the fox.

"Good morning," the little prince responded politely, although when he turned around he saw nothing.

"I am right here," the voice said, "under the apple tree."

"Who are you?" asked the little prince, and added, "You are very pretty to look at."

"I am a fox," said the fox.

"Come and play with me," proposed the little prince. "I am so unhappy."

「我不能跟你一起玩，」狐狸說：「我沒有被馴養。」

「啊！真抱歉。」小王子說。

他想了想，又說：

「什麼是『馴養』？」

「你不住在這裡。」狐狸說：「你在找什麼？」

「我在找人類。」小王子說：「什麼是『馴養』？」

"I cannot play with you," the fox said. "I am not tamed."

"Ah! Please excuse me," said the little prince.

But, after some thought, he added:

"What does that mean—'tame'?"

"You do not live here," said the fox. "What is it that you are looking for?"

"I am looking for men," said the little prince. "What does that mean—'tame'?"

「人類，」狐狸說：「他們有槍，他們還會打獵，眞是煩人！他們也養雞，這是他們唯一的優點。你是來找雞嗎？」

「不，」小王子說：「我在找朋友。什麼是『馴養』？」

「這是一件大家早就忘記的事情，」狐狸說：「馴養的意思是『建立關係』。」

「建立關係？」

「沒錯，」狐狸說。

「對我來說，你不過是一個小男孩，就像其他千千萬萬個小男孩一樣。我不需要你，你也不需要我。在你眼裡，我不過是一隻狐狸，和其他千千萬萬隻狐狸沒什麼兩樣。可是，如果你馴養了我，我們就會需要彼此的存在。對我來說，你會是世界上獨一無二的你；對你來說，我也會是世界上獨一無二的我。」

"Men," said the fox. "They have guns, and they hunt. It is very disturbing. They also raise chickens. These are their only interests. Are you looking for chickens?"

"No," said the little prince. "I am looking for friends. What does that mean— 'tame'?"

"It is an act too often neglected," said the fox. It means to establish ties."

"'To establish ties'?"

"Just that," said the fox. "

To me, you are still nothing more than a little boy who is just like a hundred thousand other little boys. And I have no need of you. And you, on your part, have no need of me. To you, I am nothing more than a fox like a hundred thousand other foxes.

But if you tame me, then we shall need each other. To me, you will be unique in all the world. To you, I shall be unique in all the world…"

「我開始有點懂了。」小王子說：「有一朵花……我想，她馴養了我……」

「沒什麼不可能的。」狐狸說：「在地球上什麼怪事都有可能發生……」

「哦，這不是發生在地球上的事。」小王子說。

狐狸十分感興趣。

「在另一個星球上？」

「是。」

「在那個星球上，有獵人嗎？」「沒有。」

「太有趣了！那有雞嗎？」

「沒有。」

「沒有什麼是完美的。」狐狸嘆了口氣道。

"It is possible," said the fox. "On the Earth one sees all sorts of things."

"Oh, but this is not on the Earth!" said the little prince.

The fox seemed perplexed, and very curious.

"On another planet?"

"Yes."

"Are there hunters on this planet?"

"No."

"Ah, that is interesting! Are there chickens?"

"No."

"Nothing is perfect," sighed the fox.

但狐狸又回到原先的話題：

　　「我的生活非常單調。我抓雞，人抓我。每隻雞都一模一樣，每個人也都一模一樣。所以我開始覺得無聊了。

　　「但你要是馴養了我，我的生活就會閃閃發亮。

But he came back to his idea.

"My life is very monotonous," the fox said. "I hunt chickens; men hunt me. All the chickens are just alike, and all the men are just alike. And, in consequence, I am a little bored.

"But if you tame me, it will be as if the sun came to shine on my life .

「我會記住你的腳步聲，跟其他人沒有半點相同。其他人的腳步聲會讓我匆忙躲到地洞裡，你的腳步聲卻會像天籟呼喚我從洞裡出來。

「你看！看到那邊的麥田了嗎？我不吃麵包，小麥對我一點用處也沒有，麥田對我毫無意義。這有點悲哀。但是你擁有一頭金髮，你要是馴養了我，這將變得多麼美妙！

「每次看到金色的小麥，我就會想起你。而且我會愛上風吹拂小麥的聲音……」

"I shall know the sound of a step that will be different from all the others. Other steps send me hurrying back underneath the ground. Yours will call me, like music, out of my burrow.

"And then look: you see the grain-fields down yonder? I do not eat bread. Wheat is of no use to me. The wheat fields have nothing to say to me. And that is sad. But you have hair that is the colour of gold. Think how wonderful that will be when you have tamed me!

"The grain, which is also golden, will bring me back the thought of you. And I shall love to listen to the wind in the wheat…"

狐狸不再開口，盯著小王子看了很久很久。

「請你馴養我吧！」他說。

「我很樂意，」小王子回答：「可是我沒有多少時間了。我要尋找朋友，還有很多事情等著我去了解。」

「你只有先馴養了事物之後，才能了解他們。」狐狸說：「人不再花時間了解任何事物，他們只會跑到商店裡買現成的東西。但是世上沒有一間店在出售友情，所以人也不再有朋友這種東西。如果你想要一個朋友，就馴養我吧！」

The fox gazed at the little prince, for a long time.

"Please—tame me!" he said.

"I want to, very much," the little prince replied. "But I have not much time. I have friends to discover, and a great many things to understand."

"One only understands the things that one tames," said the fox. "Men have no more time to understand anything. They buy things all ready made at the shops. But there is no shop anywhere where one can buy friendship, and so men have no friends any more. If you want a friend, tame me…"

「那馴養，該做些什麼呢？」小王子問。

「你要很有耐心。」狐狸答道：「一開始你要坐在草叢間，跟我稍微有點距離。我會用眼角餘光看看你，你就沉默別說話。話語是誤解的源頭。不過，每天你都要坐得近一點……」

第二天，小王子來了。

「你最好每天都同一個時間來。」

狐狸說：「比如說，你固定下午四點來，那我從三點開始就會高興期待。越是快到你來的時刻，我就越覺得幸福。一到四點，我會坐立難安，我會發現幸福的代價是什麼。

「但是，如果你愛什麼時候來就什麼時候來，我永遠都不知道要在什麼時候準備好迎接你……我們應該堅守一定的儀式。」

"What must I do, to tame you?" asked the little prince.

"You must be very patient," replied the fox. "First you will sit down at a little distance from me — like that — in the grass. I shall look at you out of the corner of my eye, and you will say nothing. Words are the source of misunderstandings. But you will sit a little closer to me, every day…"

The next day the little prince came back.

"It would have been better to come back at the same hour," said the fox. "If, for example, you come at four o'clock in the afternoon, then at three o'clock I shall begin to be happy. I shall feel happier and happier as the hour advances. At four o'clock, I shall already be worrying and jumping about. I shall show you how happy I am!

"But if you come at just any time, I shall never know at what hour my heart is to be ready to greet you… One must observe the proper rites…"

「什麼是儀式？」小王子問道。

「這也是大家早就忘記的事情。」狐狸說：「儀式會讓某一天不同於其他日子，讓某個時刻不同於其他時刻。比如，那些獵人就有一個儀式。他們每個星期四都跟村子裡的女孩跳舞。

「於是，星期四對我來說就是一個美好的日子！我可以漫步走到葡萄園那麼遠，都沒有危險。如果獵人隨便什麼時候都去跳舞，每天都差不多，那我也不會有假日了。」

就這樣，小王子馴養了狐狸。

當小王子離開的時刻即將到來……

"What is a rite?" asked the little prince.

"Those also are actions too often neglected," said the fox. "They are what make one day different from other days, one hour from other hours. There is a rite, for example, among my hunters. Every Thursday they dance with the village girls.

"So Thursday is a wonderful day for me! I can take a walk as far as the vineyards. But if the hunters danced at just any time, every day would be like every other day, and I should never have any vacation at all."

So the little prince tamed the fox.

And when the hour of his departure drew near…

「啊！」狐狸說：「我要哭了。」

「這都是你的錯，」小王子說：「我從來都不想傷害你，可是你卻要我馴養你……」

「就是這樣。」狐狸說。

「可是你要哭了！」小王子說。

「就是這樣。」狐狸說。

「這對你一點好處也沒有。」

「看那小麥的顏色，我並非一無所獲。」狐狸說。他又接著說：「再去看看那些玫瑰花吧。你現在應該可以明白，你的花確實是世界上獨一無二的。然後再回來跟我道別，到那時我會送你一個祕密作為禮物。」

"Ah," said the fox, "I shall cry."

"It is your own fault," said the little prince. "I never wished you any sort of harm; but you wanted me to tame you…"

"Yes, that is so," said the fox.

"But now you are going to cry!" said the little prince.

"Yes, that is so," said the fox.

"Then it has done you no good at all!"

"It has done me good," said the fox, "because of the color of the wheat fields." And then he added:

"Go and look again at the roses. You will understand now that yours is unique in all the world. Then come back to say goodbye to me, and I will make you a present of a secret."

小王子去看那些玫瑰。

「你們跟我的玫瑰一丁點也不像，」小王子對眾多玫瑰花說：「你們什麼都不是。沒有人馴養過你們，你們也沒有馴養過任何人。你們就像我第一次見到的狐狸一樣，他只是千千萬萬隻狐狸中的其中一隻。但是我們成了朋友，所以他現在是世界上獨一無二的狐狸了。」

這些玫瑰花十分困窘。

「你們很美麗，但是也很空虛。」

小王子繼續說：「沒有誰會為你們赴死。當然，一個普通的路人或許會覺得我的玫瑰花跟你們長得一模一樣。可是，單單她一朵花就比你們全部加起來更重要，

The little prince went away, to look again at the roses.

"You are not at all like my rose," he said. "As yet you are nothing. No one has tamed you, and you have tamed no one. You are like my fox when I first knew him. He was only a fox like a hundred thousand other foxes. But I have made him my friend, and now he is unique in all the world."

And the roses were very much embarrassed.

"You are beautiful, but you are empty," he went on.

"One could not die for you. To be sure, an ordinary passerby would think that my rose looked just like you—the rose that belongs to me. But in herself alone she is more important than all the hundreds of you other roses:

「因為是她我才天天澆水，

「因為是她我才小心翼翼拿玻璃罩蓋住，

「因為是她我才用屏風遮蔽強風，

「因為是她我才耐心除掉她身上的毛毛蟲（只留下兩三隻好變成蝴蝶），因為是她我才聽她發牢騷、聽她自吹自擂，甚至有時候一言不發。

「因為她是我的玫瑰。」

他回到狐狸身邊。

「再見。」小王子說。

「再見，」狐狸說：「我的祕密非常簡單：光用眼睛，看不見真正重要的東西。唯有用心，才能看得清楚透澈。」

"because it is she that I have watered;

"because it is she that I have put under the glass globe;

"because it is she that I have sheltered behind the screen;

"because it is for her that I have killed the caterpillars (except the two or three that we saved to become butterflies);

"because it is she that I have listened to, when she grumbled, or boasted, or even sometimes when she said nothing.

"Because she is my rose.

And he went back to meet the fox.

"Goodbye," he said.

"Goodbye," said the fox. "And now here is my secret, a very simple secret: It is only with the heart that one can see rightly; what is essential is invisible to the eye."

「唯有用心，才能看得清楚透澈。」小王子重複了一次，這樣才能牢牢記在心裡。

「就是因爲你在玫瑰身上花了這麼多時間，你的玫瑰才會變得如此重要。」

「就是因爲你在玫瑰身上花了這麼多時間……」小王子又重複一遍，這樣才能牢牢記在心裡。

「人類早就忘記這個道理，」狐狸說：「可是，你絕不能忘記。你永遠都要對你馴養的一切負責。你要對你的玫瑰負責……」

「我要對我的玫瑰負責……」小王子又重複一遍，這樣才能牢牢記在心裡。

"What is essential is invisible to the eye," the little prince repeated, so that he would be sure to remember.

"It is the time you have wasted for your rose that makes your rose so important."

"It is the time I have wasted for my rose —" said the little prince, so that he would be sure to remember.

"Men have forgotten this truth," said the fox. "But you must not forget it. You become responsible, forever, for what you have tamed. You are responsible for your rose..."

"I am responsible for my rose," the little prince repeated, so that he would be sure to remember.

「你好。」小王子說。

「你好。」鐵路工人說。

「你在這裡做什麼？」小王子問。

「我把旅客分批，每千人一批。」鐵路工人說：「車廂載滿了人就出發，有的時候往右，有的時候往左。」

然後一列燈火通明的快車匆匆而過，雷鳴般地轟隆隆響，鐵道工人的房子都震動了起來。

「這些火車真忙呀，」小王子說：「他們在找什麼嗎？」

「連管火車頭的人也不知道。」鐵路工人說。

第二列燈火通明的快車往反方向風馳電掣而過。

"Good morning," said the little prince.

"Good morning," said the railway switchman.

"What do you do here?" the little prince asked.

"I sort out travelers, in bundles of a thousand," said the switchman. *"I send off the trains that carry them; now to the right, now to the left."*

And a brilliantly lighted express train shook the switchman's cabin as it rushed by with a roar like thunder.

"They are in a great hurry," said the little prince. *"What are they looking for?"*

"Not even the locomotive engineer knows that," said the switchman.

And a second brilliantly lighted express thundered by, in the opposite direction.

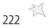

「他們馬上就回來了？」小王子問。

「他們不是之前那批人。」鐵路工人說，「這是兩列對開的火車。」

「他們不滿意原先住的地方嗎？」

「人永遠都不會安於自己原先待著的地方。」鐵路工人說。

然後第三列燈火通明的快車又轟隆隆經過。

「他們在追第一批旅客嗎？」小王子問。

「他們並不是在追逐什麼。」鐵路工人說：「他們要不是睡著了，不然就是還沒睡著在打哈欠。只有孩子會把鼻子貼在車窗上往外看。」

「只有孩子知道他們在找的是什麼。」小王子說：「他們會花時間在一個布娃娃身上，而布娃娃對他們來說就會變成很重要的東西。如果誰搶了他們的布娃娃，他們會大哭……」

「他們真幸運。」鐵路工人說。

"Are they coming back already?" demanded the little prince.

"These are not the same ones," said the switchman. "It is an exchange."

"Were they not satisfied where they were?" asked the little prince.

"No one is ever satisfied where he is," said the switchman.

And they heard the roaring thunder of a third brilliantly lighted express.

"Are they pursuing the first travelers?" demanded the little prince.

"They are pursuing nothing at all," said the switchman. "They are asleep in there, or if they are not asleep they are yawning. Only the children are flattening their noses against the windowpanes."

"Only the children know what they are looking for," said the little prince. "They waste their time over a rag doll and it becomes very important to them; and if anybody takes it away from them, they cry..."

"They are lucky," the switchman said.

23

「你好。」小王子說。

「你好。」小販說道。

這是個專門賣一種止渴藥丸的小販。只要吞一粒，你一個星期都不會覺得口渴。

「爲什麼你要賣這個東西？」小王子問。

「因爲這些藥丸可以節省非常非常多的時間。」

小販說：「專家已經計算過了，吃一顆藥丸，你每個星期能省下五十三分鐘。」

「那這五十三分鐘要做什麼？」

「愛怎麼用都可以……」

小王子喃喃自語說：「如果我有多出來的五十三分鐘，我會悠閒地漫步往泉水走去。」

"Good morning," said the little prince.

"Good morning," said the merchant.

This was a merchant who sold pills that had been invented to quench thirst. You need only swallow one pill a week, and you would feel no need of anything to drink.

"Why are you selling those?" asked the little prince.

"Because they save a tremendous amount of time," said the merchant. "Computations have been made by experts. With these pills, you save fifty-three minutes in every week."

"And what do I do with those fifty-three minutes?"

"Anything you like…"

"As for me," said the little prince to himself, "if I had fifty-three minutes to spend as I liked, I should walk at my leisure toward a spring of fresh water."

24

這是飛機在沙漠失事以來的第八天。我聽著小販的故事，嚥下了我身上僅有的最後一滴水。

「啊！」我對小王子說：「你這些回憶真是迷人。可惜，我的飛機還沒修好。

我沒有水可以喝了，如果我能夠悠閒地漫步往泉水走去，我一定會非常非常高興！」

小王子對我說：「我的朋友狐狸……」

「我的小人兒，狐狸發生什麼事現在都不重要了！」

「為什麼？」

「因為我們馬上就要渴死了。」

It was now the eighth day since I had had my accident in the desert, and I had listened to the story of the merchant as I was drinking the last drop of my water supply.

"Ah," I said to the little prince, "these memories of yours are very charming; but I have not yet succeeded in repairing my plane;

I have nothing more to drink; and I, too, should be very happy if I could walk at my leisure toward a spring of fresh water!"

"My friend the fox…" the little prince said to me.

"My dear little man, this is no longer a matter that has anything to do with the fox!"

"Why not?"

"Because I am about to die of thirst…"

他沒有跟上我的想法，回答我說：

　　「就算快死了，曾經交過一個朋友也算好事啊！比如說我，我就因為跟狐狸交朋友而覺得很開心……」

　　「他沒想到這有多兇險。」我心想：「他沒有餓過渴過。只要一點點陽光，他就滿足了……」

　　他看著我，回答了我的心裡話：

　　「我也渴了……我們去找一口井吧……」

He did not follow my reasoning, and he answered me:

"It is a good thing to have had a friend, even if one is about to die. I, for instance, am very glad to have had a fox as a friend…"

"He has no way of guessing the danger," I said to myself. "He has never been either hungry or thirsty. A little sunshine is all he needs…"

But he looked at me steadily, and replied to my thought:

"I am thirsty, too. Let us look for a well…"

我擺出一副疲倦的模樣。在看不到盡頭的大沙漠上漫無目地找一口水井，實在太荒謬了。儘管如此，我們還是出發去找水井了。

　　我們用盡力氣靜靜地走了好幾個小時以後，天色漸暗，星星開始在天空中閃爍。我因為太渴開始有點發燒，我望著這些星星彷彿身在夢中。小王子最後說的那句話在我的腦海中迴盪。

　　「你也會覺得渴嗎？」我問他。

　　他並不回答我的問題，只是對我說：

　　「水對心靈也是很好的……」

　　我不懂他這話是什麼意思，但我沒說什麼。我很明白問也沒有用。

　　他累了，就地坐下。我坐在他的身邊。一陣沉默過後，他開口：

　　「這些星星很美，是因為一朵看不見的花……」

I made a gesture of weariness. It is absurd to look for a well, at random, in the immensity of the desert. But nevertheless we started walking.

When we had trudged along for several hours, in silence, the darkness fell, and the stars began to come out. Thirst had made me a little feverish, and I looked at them as if I were in a dream. The little prince's last words came reeling back into my memory:

"Then you are thirsty, too?" I demanded.

But he did not reply to my question. He merely said to me:

"Water may also be good for the heart..."

I did not understand this answer, but I said nothing. I knew very well that it was impossible to cross-examine him.

He was tired. He sat down. I sat down beside him. And, after a little silence, he spoke again:

"The stars are beautiful, because of a flower that cannot be seen."

我回答：「嗯。」沒多說什麼，我默默看著月光下沙漠的皺褶。

「沙漠很美。」他又說。

確實如此。我一直很喜歡沙漠。坐在沙丘上，什麼都看不見，什麼都聽不見。但是一片寂靜當中，卻有什麼正在跳動、發光⋯⋯

「沙漠如此美麗，就是因爲在某個角落裡藏著一口水井⋯⋯」

我很驚訝，突然明白沙漠裡爲何會閃爍著謎樣的光芒。我小的時候曾經住在一個古老的房子裡，傳說房子裡埋著一個寶藏。當然，沒人知道該怎麼去找這個寶藏，可能根本連找都沒人去找過。但是這讓整個房子產生了一股魅力。我家的房子在心底藏著一個祕密⋯⋯

我對小王子說：「沒錯，無論房子、星星，還是沙漠，它們之所以動人都是因爲它們擁有眼睛看不到的東西！」

I replied, "Yes, that is so." And, without saying anything more, I looked across the ridges of sand that were stretched out before us in the moonlight.

"The desert is beautiful," the little prince added.

And that was true. I have always loved the desert. One sits down on a desert sand dune, sees nothing, hears nothing. Yet through the silence something throbs, and gleams...

"What makes the desert beautiful," said the little prince, "is that somewhere it hides a well..."

I was astonished by a sudden understanding of that mysterious radiation of the sands. When I was a little boy I lived in an old house, and legend told us that a treasure was buried there. To be sure, no one had ever known how to find it; perhaps no one had ever even looked for it. But it cast an enchantment over that house. My home was hiding a secret in the depths of its heart...

"Yes," I said to the little prince. "The house, the stars, the desert—what gives them their beauty is something that is invisible!"

「我眞高興，你的想法跟我的狐狸一樣。」小王子說。

小王子睡著了，我抱起他又開始往前走。我很感動，彷彿我抱著的是一個易碎的珍寶。甚至在地球上沒什麼比他更脆弱的了。

月光下我看著他蒼白的額頭、緊閉的雙眼、隨風飄動的髮絲，然後我心想：「我看到的不過是個外殼。光用眼睛，看不見眞正重要的東西……」

他的嘴微微張開似笑非笑，我心裡又想：「熟睡的小王子之所以能讓我深深感動，是因爲他對那朵花的一心一意，是因爲那朵花像盞燈火照亮了他整個人，卽使在小王子睡著的時候也是如此……」我覺得他變得更脆弱了。我得保護他，彷彿他就是燭火，一陣風吹過就熄滅了……

就這麼走著走著，天空微微發亮的時候，我發現了一口水井。

"I am glad," he said, "that you agree with my fox."

As the little prince dropped off to sleep, I took him in my arms and set out walking once more. I felt deeply moved, and stirred. It seemed to me that I was carrying a very fragile treasure. It seemed to me, even, that there was nothing more fragile on all Earth.

In the moonlight I looked at his pale forehead, his closed eyes, his locks of hair that trembled in the wind, and I said to myself: "What I see here is nothing but a shell. What is most important is invisible…"

As his lips opened slightly with the suspicious of a half-smile, I said to myself, again: "What moves me so deeply, about this little prince who is sleeping here, is his loyalty to a flower — the image of a rose that shines through his whole being like the flame of a lamp, even when he is asleep…" And I felt him to be more fragile still. I felt the need of protecting him, as if he himself were a flame that might be extinguished by a little puff of wind…

And, as I walked on so, I found the well, at daybreak.

25

「那些人擠進快車裡，卻不知道自己在尋找什麼。所以他們整日忙東忙西，忙得團團轉……」小王子說。

他又加了一句：

「不值得……」

我們終於找到的這口井，跟撒哈拉沙漠裡的那些井不一樣。撒哈拉沙漠裡的井不過是在沙漠中挖個洞。我們找到的井則是跟村莊裡的水井很像，但是這裡並沒有任何村莊，我以為自己在做夢。

「真不尋常，」我對小王子說：「打水用的滑輪、水桶、繩子……所有東西都準備好了……」

"Men," said the little prince, "set out on their way in express trains, but they do not know what they are looking for. Then they rush about, and get excited, and turn round and round…"

And he added:

"It is not worth the trouble…"

The well that we had come to was not like the wells of the Sahara. The wells of the Sahara are mere holes dug in the sand. This one was like a well in a village. But there was no village here, and I thought I must be dreaming…

"It is strange," I said to the little prince. "Everything is ready for use: the pulley, the bucket, the rope…"

他笑了，拿起繩子，轉動滑輪。滑輪像個很久沒被風吹過的破舊風向儀一般，呻吟了起來。

「聽到了嗎？」小王子說：「我們喚醒了這口井，它開始唱歌了……」

我不想讓他因為打水而覺得疲累。

我對他說：「讓我來吧。這對你來說太重了。」

我緩慢拉起水桶，穩穩地放在井邊。耳邊滑輪的歌聲仍在迴響，我彷彿還看得到井裡水面上的波光粼粼。

「我渴望這口井的水。」小王子說：「讓我喝一些……」

我突然明白了他在尋找的是什麼！

He laughed, touched the rope, and set the pulley to working. And the pulley moaned, like an old weathervane which the wind has long since forgotten.

"Do you hear?" said the little prince. "We have wakened the well, and it is singing…"

I did not want him to tire himself with the rope.

"Leave it to me," I said. "It is too heavy for you."

I hoisted the bucket slowly to the edge of the well and set it there—happy, tired as I was, over my achievement. The song of the pulley was still in my ears, and I could see the sunlight shimmer in the still trembling water.

"I am thirsty for this water," said the little prince. "Give me some of it to drink…"

And I understood what he had been looking for.

我提起水桶放在他的嘴邊。他喝著水閉上了眼睛，好像這水像節慶一般美好。

　　這水確實與普通的食物不同，它誕生自星夜下的長途跋涉，誕生自滑輪的歌聲中，誕生自我雙手的努力。

　　它像一件禮物足以豐富心靈。當我還是個小男孩時，聖誕樹上的小燈泡、午夜彌撒的樂聲、眾人甜滋滋的微笑，正是因為這一切我的聖誕禮物才會那麼美好。

I raised the bucket to his lips. He drunk, his eyes closed. It was as sweet as some special festival treat.

This water was indeed a different thing from ordinary nourishment. Its sweetness was born of the walk under the stars, the song of the pulley, the effort of my arms.

It was good for the heart, like a present. When I was a little boy, the lights of the Christmas tree, the music of the Midnight Mass, the tenderness of smiling faces, used to make up, so, the radiance of the gifts I received.

「地球上的人可以在一個花園裡種下五千朵玫瑰。」小王子說：「但是他們在那裡卻找不到自己尋求的東西……」

「他們找不到的。」我答道。

「可是他們尋找的東西其實是可以從一朵玫瑰花或一點水當中找到的……」

「的確。」我回答道。

小王子加了一句：

「用眼睛什麼也看不到。要用心靈去尋找才行。」

我喝下水，呼吸也變得輕盈。破曉的日光映照在沙漠上如蜜一般。這蜜色般的光彩讓我覺得快樂。但是為什麼這也讓我覺得悲傷……

"The men where you live," said the little prince, "raise five thousand roses in the same garden — and they do not find in it what they are looking for."

"They do not find it," I replied.

"And yet what they are looking for could be found in one single rose, or in a little water."

"Yes, that is true," I said.

And the little prince added:

"But the eyes are blind. One must look with the heart…"

I had drunk the water. I breathed easily. At sunrise the sand is the color of honey. And that honey color was making me happy, too. What brought me, then, this sense of grief?

小王子再次坐在我身邊，輕輕地對我說：「你應該實現你的諾言。」

「什麼諾言？」

「你知道……替我的羊畫一個嘴套……我得對我的花負責！」

於是我從口袋裡拿出圖畫的草稿。小王子一張張看過，笑著說：

「你把猴麵包樹畫得有點像高麗菜……」

「哦！」

我一直以自己畫的猴麵包樹為傲！

「你把狐狸的耳朵……畫得有點像角……而且太長了！」

他又笑了。

「這不公平啊，小王子。」我說：「我只會畫吃飽喝足的蟒蛇跟看得見肚子裡東西的蟒蛇。」

"You must keep your promise," said the little prince, softly, as he sat down beside me once more.

"What promise?"

"You know—a muzzle for my sheep... I am responsible for this flower..."

I took my rough drafts of drawings out of my pocket. The little prince looked them over, and laughed as he said:

"Your baobabs—they look a little like cabbages."

"Oh!"

I had been so proud of my baobabs!

"Your fox—his ears look a little like horns; and they are too long."

And he laughed again.

"You are not fair, little prince," I said. "I don't know how to draw anything except boa constrictors from the outside and boa constrictors from the inside."

「哦！這就夠了。」他說：「孩子都會看懂的。」

我用鉛筆畫了個嘴套。當我拿給小王子的時候，心裡一陣撕扯：

「你有什麼計畫是我不知道的⋯⋯」

他沒有回答我，只是對我說：

「你知道的，我降落在地球上⋯⋯到明天就滿一年了⋯⋯」

他沉默了一會兒，繼續說道：

「我當時就降落在附近⋯⋯」

他臉紅了。

"Oh, that will be all right," he said, "children understand."

So then I made a pencil sketch of a muzzle. And as I gave it to him my heart was torn.

"You have plans that I do not know about," I said.

But he did not answer me. He said to me, instead:

"You know—my descent to the earth... Tomorrow will be its anniversary."

Then, after a silence, he went on:

"I came down very near here."

And he flushed.

不知道為什麼，我心裡又是一陣悲傷。不過，我突然想起一個問題：

「一個星期以前你獨自一人在遠離人煙千里的地方行走，那天早上我遇到你應該不是偶然的吧？那時你是準備回到降落的地點去？」

小王子又臉紅了。

我有些猶豫地加了一句：

「或許是因為滿一年的緣故……？」小王子還是臉紅了。他從來不回答問題，但是當人臉紅的時候，不就等於是默認了？

「啊！」我對他說：「我怕……」

但他卻答道：「現在你該去工作了。你該回去修引擎了。我在這裡等你，明天晚上你再過來……」

但我不放心。我想起狐狸的話。如果被馴養了，可能會想哭……

And once again, without understanding why, I had a queer sense of sorrow. One question, however, occurred to me:

"Then it was not by chance that on the morning when I first met you—a week ago—you were strolling along like that, all alone, a thousand miles from any inhabited region? You were on the your back to the place where you landed?"

The little prince flushed again.

And I added, with some hesitancy:

"Perhaps it was because of the anniversary?"

The little prince flushed once more. He never answered questions—but when one flushes does that not mean "Yes"?

"Ah," I said to him, "I am a little frightened…"

But he interrupted me.

"Now you must work. You must return to your engine. I will be waiting for you here. Come back tomorrow evening…"

But I was not reassured. I remembered the fox. One runs the risk of weeping a little, if one lets himself be tamed…

26

　　水井的旁邊有一道破敗的舊石牆。隔天晚上我工作結束回來的時候，遠遠就看到小王子坐在石牆上，兩腿晃呀晃的。我聽見他在說話。

　　「你忘了？」他說：「不是這裡。」

　　應該有另一個聲音與他對答，因為小王子又說：

　　「不，不，時間沒錯，但不是在這裡……」

　　我繼續走向石牆，卻還是看不到人，也聽不見任何聲音。可是小王子又答道：

　　「……當然。你會在沙上看到我來時的足跡，在那裡等我吧。今晚我會去跟你會合。」

　　我走到離石牆二十公尺遠的地方，卻還是什麼也看不見。

Beside the well there was the ruin of an old stone wall. When I came back from my work, the next evening, I saw from some distance away my little price sitting on top of a wall, with his feet dangling. And I heard him say:

"Then you don't remember. This is not the exact spot."

Another voice must have answered him, for he replied to it:

"Yes, yes! It is the right day, but this is not the place."

I continued my walk toward the wall. At no time did I see or hear anyone. The little prince, however, replied once again:

"...Exactly. You will see where my track begins, in the sand. You have nothing to do but wait for me there. I shall be there tonight."

I was only twenty metres from the wall, and I still saw nothing.

小王子沉默了一陣，又開口說：

「你的毒液夠毒嗎？你確定我不會痛苦太久？」

我停下腳步，心彷彿被撕碎了一般。但我還是不懂到底發生了什麼事。

「你走吧。我要下來了！」小王子說。

我跟著垂下眼看向石牆底，嚇得我跳了起來。在我眼前，一條在三十秒內就可以置人於死地的黃蛇，正面對著小王子。我把手伸進口袋拿出手槍，跑了過去。可是一聽到我的腳步聲，那條蛇就像一道乾枯的水流，穿過石頭的縫隙，慢慢鑽進沙裡消失不見，一路上發出金屬碰撞般的叮咚聲響。

我到牆邊的時候，剛好接住這位小人兒。他的臉色如雪一般蒼白。

「這是怎麼回事？」我問：「你居然在跟蛇說話！」

After a silence the little prince spoke again:

"You have good poison? You are sure that it will not make me suffer too long?"

I stopped in my tracks, my heart torn asunder; but still I did not understand.

"Now go away," said the little prince. "I want to get down from the wall."

I dropped my eyes, then, to the foot of the wall…and I leaped into the air. There before me, facing the little prince, was one of those yellow snakes that take just thirty seconds to bring your life to an end. Even as I was digging into my pocked to get out my revolver I made a running step back. But, at the noise I made, the snake let himself flow easily across the sand like the dying spray of a fountain, and, in no apparent hurry, disappeared, with a light metallic sound, among the stones.

I reached the wall just in time to catch my little man in my arms; his face was white as snow.

"What does this mean?" I demanded. "Why are you talking with snakes?"

我鬆開他始終戴在身上的金色圍巾。我用水沾濕他的太陽穴，也給他喝了些水。我什麼問題也不敢問。他認真地看著我，伸出雙臂摟著我的頸項。他的心跳十分微弱，跟一隻被來福槍射中而瀕臨死亡的鳥一樣。

　　「你找到引擎出的問題在哪裡了，我很開心。」

　　他說：「你馬上就可以回家了……」

　　「你怎麼知道！」

　　我就是來告訴他，在不抱任何期待的情況下，我成功修好引擎了。

　　他沒回答我的問題，只是接著說：

　　「我今天，也要回家了……」

　　然後，他難過地說：

　　「我回家的路太遠……也太艱難了……」

I had loosened the golden muffler that he always wore. I had moistened his temples, and had given him some water to drink. And now I did not dare ask him any more questions. He looked at me very gravely, and put his arms around my neck. I felt his heart beating like the heart of a dying bird, shot with someone's rifle...

"I am glad that you have found what was the matter with your engine," he said. "Now you can go back home."

"How do you know about that?"

I was just coming to tell him that my work had been successful, beyond anything that I had dared to hope.

He made no answer to my question, but he added:

"I, too, am going back home today..."

Then, sadly —

"It is much farther... it is much more difficult..."

我相當明白，有些不對勁的事正要發生。我緊緊抱著他，好像他是個嬰兒。可是他好似正在迅速往深淵跌落，我想牢牢抓住他，卻是徒勞無功……

他的眼神非常非常認真，視線落在遠方。

「我有你畫給我的羊、羊住的箱子和嘴套……」

他露出一個悲傷的微笑。

我等了很久，感覺到他身體漸漸暖和起來。

「我親愛的小人兒，你怕了……」

毫無疑問，他懼怕了。但他淺淺地笑著說：

「今晚，我會比現在更加害怕……」

I realized realised clearly that something extraordinary was happening. I was holding him close in my arms as if he were a little child; and yet it seemed to me that he was rushing headlong toward an abyss from which I could do nothing to restrain him…

His look was very serious, like some one lost far away.

"I have your sheep. And I have the sheep's box. And I have the muzzle…"

And he gave me a sad smile.

I waited a long time. I could see that he was reviving little by little.

"Dear little man," I said to him, "you are afraid…"

He was afraid, there was no doubt about that. But he laughed lightly.

"I shall be much more afraid this evening…"

又一次，我預感有什麼無法挽救的事情將要發生，全身彷彿落入冰窖一般。我一想到再也聽不到他的笑聲，就難過得不能自已。他的笑聲對我來說，就像沙漠中的清泉。

「小人兒，」我說：「我想再聽到你笑……」

但他對我說：

「到今晚就剛好一整年了。我的星球會正好走到我去年降落地點的正上方……」

「小人兒，」我說：「告訴我這只是一場噩夢。這條蛇、你和他的約定，還有星星，全都是噩夢吧？」

但是他並沒有答應我的要求，只是對我說：

「光用眼睛，看不見真正重要的東西……」

「我知道……」

Once again I felt myself frozen by the sense of something irreparable. And I knew that I could not bear the thought of never hearing that laughter any more. For me, it was like a spring of fresh water in the desert.

"Little man," I said, "I want to hear you laugh again."

But he said to me:

"Tonight, it will be a year... my star, then, can be found right above the place where I came to the Earth, a year ago..."

"Little man," I said, "tell me that it is only a bad dream, this affair of the snake, and the meeting-place, and the star..."

But he did not answer my plea. He said to me, instead: "The thing that is important is the thing that is not seen..."

"Yes, I know..."

「就像花。如果你愛上了一朵長在星星上的花，到晚上你只要望著天空就會覺得甜蜜。好像每顆星星上都開著花。」

「我知道……」

「就像水。因為那滾輪和那條繩子，你給我喝的水就像天籟……你記得嗎？……那水多麼香甜……」

「我知道……」

「到晚上，你會抬頭望著星星。我的星球太小了，所以我沒辦法指給你看我的星星在哪裡。其實這樣更好。在你眼裡我的星星就是這眾多星星裡的一顆。你會愛上望著天空裡的每一顆星星……這些星星都會是你的朋友。然後，我還要給你一件禮物……」

他又笑了。

「小王子，我親愛的小王子，我好愛你的笑聲！」

"It is just as it is with the flower. If you love a flower that lives on a star, it is sweet to look at the sky at night. All the stars are a-bloom with flowers…"

"Yes, I know…"

"It is just as it is with the water. Because of the pulley, and the rope, what you gave me to drink was like music. You remember, how good it was."

"Yes, I know…"

"And at night you will look up at the stars. Where I live everything is so small that I cannot show you where my star is to be found. It is better, like that. My star will just be one of the stars, for you. And so you will love to watch all the stars in the heavens… they will all be your friends. And, besides, I am going to make you a present…"

He laughed again.

"Ah, little prince, dear little prince! I love to hear that laughter!"

「這就是我的禮物，僅僅如此。就像我們喝下的井水……」

「你想說什麼？」

「星星在不同的人眼裡代表的東西都不一樣。

「在旅行者眼裡，星星是嚮導。

「在其他人眼裡，星星不過是夜空中的小燈泡。

「在學者眼裡，星星是研究課題。

「在我碰到的那個商人眼裡，星星是財富。

「但是，所有的星星都是沉默的。你，只有你擁有這些星星的方式，是別人不曾有過的……」

"That is my present. Just that. It will be as it was when we drank the water…"

"What are you trying to say?"

"All men have the stars," he answered, "but they are not the same things for different people.

"For some, who are travelers, the stars are guides.

"For others they are no more than little lights in the sky.

"For others, who are scholars, they are problems . For my businessman they were wealth.

"But all these stars are silent. You—you alone—will have the stars as no one else has them…"

「你想說什麼？」

「我住在其中一顆星星上，所以我也會在其中一顆星星上笑著。所以當你望著夜空的時候，在你眼裡就像所有星星都笑了起來⋯⋯你，只有你擁有愛笑的星星！」

"What are you trying to say?"

"In one of the stars I shall be living. In one of them I shall be laughing. And so it will be as if all the stars were laughing, when you look at the sky at night… you—only you—will have stars that can laugh!"

說著說著，他又笑了起來。

「然後，在你的傷痛和緩之後（人總能自行痊癒），你會因為曾經認識我而感到高興。你永遠都是我的朋友。你會想跟我一起笑。你也會不時打開窗戶，尋找歡笑……你的朋友可能會被你望著天空發笑的舉動嚇傻。到時候，你可以對他們說：『沒錯，星星總是讓我發笑！』他們會以為你瘋了。這就是我的破把戲……」

他又笑了。

「彷彿我給你的不是星星，而是非常多非常多會笑的小鈴鐺……」

And he laughed again.

"And when your sorrow is comforted (time soothes all sorrows) you will be content that you have known me. You will always be my friend. You will want to laugh with me. And you will sometimes open your window, so, for that pleasure... and your friends will be properly astonished to see you laughing as you look up at the sky! Then you will say to them, 'Yes, the stars always make me laugh!' And they will think you are crazy. It will be a very shabby trick that I shall have played on you..."

And he laughed again.

"It will be as if, in place of the stars, I had given you a great number of little bells that knew how to laugh..."

他再一次笑了。不過他很快就一臉認眞地說：

「今晚⋯⋯你知道的⋯⋯不要來。」小王子說。

「我不會離開你。」

「我的樣子會看起來很痛苦⋯⋯看起來會有點像快死了。就是這樣，別來看。這不值得⋯⋯」

「我不會離開你。」

可是他卻擔心。

「告訴你這些⋯⋯也是因爲那條蛇。別被他咬了⋯⋯蛇是邪惡的生物，他會爲了好玩咬人⋯⋯」

「我不會離開你。」

但有個想法讓他稍微放心：

「他咬的第二口就沒有毒液了⋯⋯」

And he laughed again. Then he quickly became serious:

"Tonight—you know... do not come," said the little prince.

"I shall not leave you," I said.

"I shall look as if I were suffering. I shall look a little as if I were dying. It is like that. Do not come to see that. It is not worth the trouble..."

"I shall not leave you."

But he was worried.

"I tell you—it is also because of the snake. He must not bite you. Snakes—they are malicious creatures. This one might bite you just for fun..."

"I shall not leave you."

But a thought came to reassure him:

"It is true that they have no more poison for a second bite."

這天晚上，我沒看到他啓程。他一聲不響地從我身邊溜走了。當我追上他的時候，他毅然決然地快步向前走。他只對我說：

「啊，你來了……」

於是他牽著我的手，卻仍然在擔心：

「你不該來。你會難過的。我看起來會像死了，儘管這並非事實……」

我沉默不語。

「你懂的，路太遠了。我不能帶著這副身軀上路，太重了。」

我還是沉默不語。

「不過，這就像老樹皮脫落。你不必爲老樹皮傷心。」

我依然沉默不語。

That night I did not see him set out on his way. He got away from me without making a sound. When I succeeded in catching up with him he was walking along with a quick and resolute step. He said to me merely:

"Ah! You are there…"

And he took me by the hand. But he was still worrying.

"It was wrong of you to come. You will suffer. I shall look as if I were dead; and that will not be true…"

I said nothing.

"You understand… it is too far. I cannot carry this body with me. It is too heavy."

I said nothing.

"But it will be like an old abandoned shell. There is nothing sad about old shells…"

I said nothing.

他有些挫折，但又繼續努力：

「你知道，一切都會變好的。我也會望著星星。每一顆星星都會是帶著生鏽滑輪的井。每一顆星星都會倒水給我喝……」

我仍舊沉默不語。

「這會變得多好玩啊！你擁有五億個鈴鐺，而我擁有五億口水井……」

他也不再說話，因爲他在哭泣……

「就是這裡。讓我獨自上路吧。」

因爲恐懼，他坐了下來。然後又開口說：「你知道……我的花……我要對她負責！她那麼弱小！又那麼天眞！她只有四根毫無用處的刺，在全世界面前用來保護自己……」

我也坐下，因爲再也站不住了。

He was a little discouraged. But he made one more effort:

"You know, it will be very nice. I, too, shall look at the stars. All the stars will be wells with a rusty pulley. All the stars will pour out fresh water for me to drink..."

I said nothing.

"That will be so amusing! You will have five hundred million little bells, and I shall have five hundred million springs of fresh water..."

And he too said nothing more, because he was crying...

"Here it is. Let me go on by myself."

And he sat down, because he was afraid. Then he said, again:

"You know—my flower... I am responsible for her. And she is so weak! She is so naive! She has four thorns, of no use at all, to protect herself against all the world..."

I too sat down, because I was not able to stand up any longer.

「就這樣了……」

他還有點猶豫，然後站了起來。他踏出一步，我卻動彈不得。

一道黃色的光芒閃過他的腳踝，在那一瞬間他絲毫不動。他沒有喊出聲，緩緩地像棵樹一樣倒下。他倒在沙地上，沒有發出一點聲響。

"There now — that is all…"

He still hesitated a little; then he got up. He took one step. I could not move.

There was nothing but a flash of yellow close to his ankle. He remained motionless for an instant. He did not cry out. He fell as gently as a tree falls. There was not even any sound, because of the sand.

27

六年過去了……我從未把這個故事告訴別人。夥伴們看到我活著回來，都十分高興。我卻覺得悲傷，不過只跟他們解釋道：「我累了……」

現在，我的悲傷稍稍和緩。也就是說……我還沒有完全康復。可是我知道他已經回到他的星球。因為他離去的那天清晨，我沒有找到他的身軀，顯然那並不是一副沉重的身軀……此後，我就愛上在夜晚傾聽星星，彷彿是五億個鈴鐺齊響……

And now six years have already gone by...

I have never yet told this story. The companions who met me on my return were well content to see me alive. I was sad, but I told them: "I am tired."

Now my sorrow is comforted a little. That is to say—not entirely. But I know that he did go back to his planet, because I did not find his body at daybreak. It was not such a heavy body... and at night I love to listen to the stars. It is like five hundred million little bells...

但還有一件事不對勁。我畫了嘴套給小王子，卻忘了畫繫繩！他永遠都無法替羊戴上嘴套。所以我一直在想：「小王子的星球上發生什麼事了？或許羊已經一口把花吃了⋯⋯」

　　有時候我會對自己說：「一定不會發生這種事的！小王子每天晚上都會用玻璃罩蓋住他的花，而且他會小心看好他的羊⋯⋯」想到這裡，我又高興了起來，而所有的星星都在溫柔地笑著。

But there is one extraordinary thing... when I drew the muzzle for the little prince, I forgot to add the leather strap to it. He will never have been able to fasten it on his sheep. So now I keep wondering: what is happening on his planet? Perhaps the sheep has eaten the flower...

At one time I say to myself: "Surely not! The little prince shuts his flower under her glass globe every night, and he watches over his sheep very carefully..." Then I am happy. And there is sweetness in the laughter of all the stars.

但是有的時候，我又會對自己說：「難免會有疏忽的時候，一旦發生就糟糕了！要是某個晚上他忘記蓋玻璃罩，或是那頭羊偷偷溜出來……」想到這裡，所有小鈴鐺都變成淚滴了……

於是，這成了一個巨大的謎團。對喜歡小王子的人，還有我來說，如果在我們不知道的地方，那隻我們看不見的羊吃了一朵玫瑰花，或是沒吃玫瑰花，整個宇宙的樣貌就會全然改變。

看看天空，問問你自己：羊到底吃了花還是沒吃？

然後你會看到這個世界變了樣……

大人永遠不會明白這個問題有多麼重要！

But at another time I say to myself: "At some moment or other one is absent-minded, and that is enough! On some one evening he forgot the glass globe, or the sheep got out, without making any noise, in the night..." And then the little bells are changed to tears...

Here, then, is a great mystery. For you who also love the little prince, and for me, nothing in the universe can be the same if somewhere, we do not know where, a sheep that we never saw has — yes or no? — eaten a rose...

Look up at the sky. Ask yourselves: is it yes or no? Has the sheep eaten the flower? And you will see how everything changes...

And no grown-up will ever understand that this is a matter of so much importance!

對我來說，這是世界上最美麗也最傷人的地方。跟前面幾頁畫的是同一個地方，我再次畫出來，是為了讓你牢牢記住。小王子就是在這裡，降臨到地球上，也是在這裡消失無蹤。

看仔細了。有一天你到非洲沙漠旅行的時候，才能準確地認出這個地方。如果你恰巧經過這個地方，請不要匆匆走過，在那顆星星的正下方等一段時間。

要是有個小人兒笑著向你走來，並且擁有一頭金髮，他還不願意回答你的問題，你就知道他是誰了。請幫我一個忙，別讓我再次後悔。請盡快寫信告訴我，他回來了⋯⋯

This is, to me, the loveliest and saddest landscape in the world. It is the same as that on the preceding page, but I have drawn it again to impress it on your memory. It is here that the little prince appeared on Earth, and disappeared.

Look at it carefully so that you will be sure to recognize it in case you travel some day to the African desert. And, if you should come upon this spot, please do not hurry on. Wait for a time, exactly under the star. Then, if a little man appears who laughs, who has golden hair and who refuses to answer questions, you will know who he is. If this should happen, please comfort me. Send me word that he has come back……

【寫‧小王子】
透過手抄、慢讀，打開心靈的眼睛，藉由書寫，體驗「寫下來」帶來的改變

作　　　者	安東尼‧聖修伯里（Antoine de Saint-Exupéry）
譯　　　者	墨丸
封 面 設 計	比比司工作室
內 頁 構 成	陳姿秀、高巧怡
行 銷 企 劃	蕭浩仰、江紫涓
行 銷 統 籌	駱漢琦
業 務 發 行	邱紹溢
營 運 顧 問	郭其彬
責 任 編 輯	林芳吟
總 編 輯	李亞南
出　　　版	漫遊者文化事業股份有限公司
地　　　址	台北市103大同區重慶北路二段88號2樓之6
電　　　話	(02) 2715-2022
傳　　　真	(02) 2715-2021
服 務 信 箱	service@azothbooks.com
網 路 書 店	www.azothbooks.com
臉　　　書	www.facebook.com/azothbooks.read
發　　　行	大雁出版基地
地　　　址	新北市231新店區北新路三段207-3號5樓
電　　　話	02-8913-1005
訂 單 傳 真	02-8913-1056
初 版 一 刷	2024年1月
定　　　價	台幣360元

ISBN　978-986-489-894-7
有著作權‧侵害必究

國家圖書館出版品預行編目 (CIP) 資料

寫. 小王子：透過手抄、慢讀，打開心靈的眼睛，
藉由書寫, 體驗「寫下來」帶來的改變/ 安東
尼. 聖修伯里(Antoine de Saint-Exupéry) 著；
墨丸譯. -- 初版. -- 臺北市：漫遊者文化事業股
份有限公司, 2024.01
　　面； 公分
譯自：The little prince.
ISBN 978-986-489-894-7(平裝)
876.57　　　　　　　　　　112022735